Mr. One and Only

Sharon C Cooper

Published by Amaris Publishing LLC, 2023.

Mr. One and Only
By
Sharon C. Cooper

Disclaimer

Prologue

The moment Genesis Savell stepped out of her office building and onto the busy sidewalk in Midtown Atlanta, she inhaled a deep breath and released it slowly. It was late April with blue skies and a perfect seventy-five degrees.

Spring weather was almost non-existent in the city, but for the last couple of days, they'd had a taste of it. No doubt next week would be back in the eighties the way it had been the week before.

Now for coffee.

As she strolled along the semi-busy sidewalk, Genesis thought about the projects on her to-do list for the afternoon. A regular black coffee wouldn't do. She was going to need something stronger... and sweeter.

The coffee shop was only a few doors down, and the moment Genesis walked in, she inhaled deeply. The aroma alone gave her an extra pep in her step, and she quickly placed her order. A short while later, carrying an iced latte with an extra shot of espresso, she headed back towards the office.

She had barely taken three steps when she heard, "Hello, Genesis," and she froze. The voice was familiar, but the handsome man wearing an Atlanta Braves baseball cap and smiling at her wasn't. He was around six feet tall with skin the color of mocha, and an athletic build encased in a fitted T-shirt and jeans that hung low on his hips.

"You don't remember me, do you?" he said and pushed away from the brick building.

When he moved toward her, Genesis took a step back as she tried to place him. There was something familiar about him, but...

Oh, my God. "Ronnie?" she squealed.

He chuckled. "Yeah, sweet Genesis, it's me."

The smile on his face broadened, and she lunged into his arms before thinking but was careful of the coffee in her hand.

"Wow," Genesis said as they hugged. "How are you? Where have you..." Her words trailed off, and she was glad she caught herself before asking where he'd been. She knew, and memories of the scariest night of her life flooded her mind.

Genesis stiffened and pushed the memories away as she eased out of his hold.

"I got out earlier this year," Ronnie said.

The joy she felt moments ago vanished and was replaced with sorrow for their lost friendship. They'd lived in the same foster home during high school, and Ronnie had been the big brother she'd never had. He was only a few months older than her, but back then, it seemed like they were years apart.

And now here he was... sixteen years later.

Everything had changed the night he'd been arrested for armed robbery of a convenience store.

Genesis had always looked up to him and had even had a crush on him. He'd been one of her best friends... her protector. He had even saved her life. Yet, she hadn't visited or reached out to him not once in all those years.

Ronnie's gaze raked over her body before returning to her face. "It's good seeing you. You look amazing. We should catch up. Do you have time for a bite to eat?"

She glanced at the slim, platinum watch on her wrist. "Yeah, I have time. There's a cafe around the corner. Want to go there?"

"Sure. Lead the way."

A few minutes later, Ronnie pulled open the door. They ordered at the counter before finding a seat and talked like old friends. Though small talk flowed between them, Genesis found herself growing uncomfortable. Ronnie had told her that after being released from prison, he had moved into a halfway house. Now he was crashing on a sofa at a friend's apartment.

"It looks like you've done well for yourself," he said while they ate. "What did you do after you aged out?"

Genesis had been lost after aging out of foster care. At eighteen and naïve about life in general, her foster sister, Samantha, who had aged out six months earlier, took her in. They'd been roommates ever since, and Genesis wasn't sure what she would've done without Sam.

"I attended Georgia State and earned a degree in business management," she said.

She had always been book-smart and excelled in college. Once she graduated, Genesis landed a good-paying job, and she had worked for the organization for over twelve years. That was until the company was sold and she was laid off. It had taken her months to get her current position at G-spark Engineering.

As she and Ronnie chatted, it felt strange sitting across from him now that they were all grown up. He was still as good-looking but bigger, and he had an edginess about him that was probably thanks to prison.

"Why didn't you ever write to me or visit me?" Ronnie asked out of nowhere. "I sent you a letter with my address, but I never heard from you."

"I never received it," Genesis said honestly, but that guilt from earlier twisted inside of her like a double edge sword.

She probably could've gotten information on where he was serving his time, but after he'd been charged, she cut all ties. Her foster mother threatened to kick her out if she maintained contact with him. The last thing Genesis had wanted was to get moved to yet another foster home, especially since she'd been months from aging out.

The other reason she hadn't wanted anything to do with Ronnie after that night was because of the role she played in his arrest. A role that very few people knew about.

That guilt dug deeper into her gut.

"I'm sorry we lost touch," she said, "but I'm glad you're out and starting your life over."

"Yeah, now that I'm working at a body shop, I can save up some money. Me and my buddy plan to buy the business soon, and we have some other ventures in the works. So... everything is good."

As he chatted about his plans, Genesis wondered if some of his goals were a little too lofty. Especially since it sounded as if they were planning to buy the body shop in the next couple of weeks.

How was that possible considering he had just gotten out of prison? Maybe his friend had money. Or maybe the owner was giving them a good deal. Whatever the case he sounded excited, and she was happy for him.

A short while later, they finished eating and headed outside.

Genesis nervously adjusted her handbag strap on her shoulder. "It was great running into you, Ronnie. Good luck with everything."

She wasn't sure how to end their visit. Did they shake hands, or should she just give a little wave and walk away? The decision was made for her when Ronnie pulled her into a hug.

"I'm glad I ran into you, sweet Genesis," he said, holding on to her a little longer than she thought appropriate. He didn't release her until she gently pushed against his chest.

"Ronnie, take care of yourself. I wish you all the best."

He chuckled. "Damn, girl. You act like this is goodbye. I'll be seeing you around."

He winked at her, then pulled his cap low over his eyes and walked in the opposite direction that she was going.

Genesis swallowed hard. It might've been good seeing him, but she hoped to never see him again. He was part of a past that she never wanted to revisit, and that could only happen if she stayed far away from Ronnie Peterson.

Chapter One

Four weeks later...

"It doesn't matter how often I've worked on this Juneteenth event, I always learn something new," Genesis said to her coworker, Carol.

Like her, Carol Thompson was an executive assistant at G-spark Engineering Firm, and they worked in the marketing department. They had become fast friends from the moment they met.

The two of them were currently sitting in one of the conference rooms ironing out the last details of the Juneteenth gala and silent auction that would take place in a few weeks. This was Genesis's second year working on the event, but it was her first time being in charge of it. She wanted this one to be the best yet.

"I agree. I've learned so much about the holiday," Carol said as she pushed her blue-framed glasses up on her nose. "Like, I had no idea that some people refer to Juneteenth as the Second Independence Day. If that's the case, we should include fireworks. That could be a fabulous way to top off the evening. There's a huge courtyard right off the hotel ballroom and several double doors that lead out to it.

Genesis swept her micro braids up and put them into a loose ponytail on top of her head. "That's an excellent idea. I've been trying to think of a way to make this year stand out from the rest. That might do it.

"If you can get quotes from several fireworks companies, I'll see if we can squeeze it into the budget."

"Great. I'll work on that in the morning," Carol said as she jotted something down on her notepad.

"Oh, also"—Genesis snapped her fingers—"I heard back from Mr. Ray. He confirmed that he'll be auctioning off two tickets to the Atlanta Hawks' season opener. The seats are right behind the players' bench and should go for a pretty penny."

Carol's eyes lit up. "Now, if only I could afford them." She laughed, then set her pen down and rocked back in her seat. "Did you ever hear from the woman at..." A knock on the closed door interrupted her question.

"Come in," Genesis called out and stood. When the door opened, the first thing she saw was a large bouquet. "Wow, those are beautiful."

The woman who helped monitor the front desk smiled. "They are, aren't they? And they were just delivered to you," she said and handed them to Genesis before leaving the room and closing the door behind her.

Genesis couldn't hide the grin that spread across her mouth. She already knew who they were from. She set the crystal vase on the table and plucked the white envelope from the bouquet of tropical flowers.

Her smile grew as she read the note: *I'm looking forward to our date tonight. N*

"I guess boss man was thinking about you." Carol smirked. "I just want to know what you did to earn such gorgeous flowers?"

Genesis stuffed the note into her pants pocket. "My lips are sealed."

Carol grinned. "I bet that's not what you said last night."

Genesis's mouth dropped open, but she quickly closed it as heat rushed to her cheeks. She hadn't wanted anyone to know that she was dating the boss. Not just any boss, but Noah Chambers, the owner of G-spark Engineering firm—a multimillion-dollar company that was nationally known.

She didn't report directly to him, which would've been awkward, but they worked in the same building. With her office being on the third floor and his on the tenth floor—the top floor—they didn't see each other much during the day. Otherwise, she wouldn't get any work done.

She and Noah had met over a year ago while she assisted her supervisor with the plans for last year's Juneteenth celebration. Genesis could honestly say it had been love at first sight for her, but she hadn't planned on acting on her attraction to him.

Even now, her heart fluttered as she recalled how Noah asked her out for coffee several weeks after meeting. That's when she realized the attraction was mutual. Still, they hadn't started officially dating until three months ago, and it had been the best three months of her life.

"Come on, Gen. At my age, I'm living vicariously through you. Give me something," Carol pleaded.

She was in her early sixties with smooth mahogany skin, and she didn't look a day over forty. Carol didn't date much, but she typically went out with guys who were Noah's age—early forties.

The older woman was one of the sweetest people Genesis had met since being at the company. Even still, she only trusted her to a certain extent. Growing up in foster care, Genesis had learned early on that everyone couldn't be trusted, and that mentality had carried over into adulthood.

Carol patted Genesis's hand. "I see you blushing."

That made Genesis laugh. Her skin tone was deep brown, and there was no way Carol could spot a blush on her cheeks.

"I'm sorry," the woman continued. "I don't mean to make you uncomfortable. You're entitled to your secrets, but I'm hoping the two of you end up married. You're a beautiful couple."

Genesis gave her a small smile. The only reason Carol knew about her dating Noah was because they had run into her one evening while out to dinner. That had been a month ago, and Carol promised to keep what she'd seen quiet, but it was conversations like this one that made Genesis uncomfortable with it all.

In the beginning, she hesitated when Noah asked her out. Not just because he was the big boss, but also because he was nine years older than her thirty-three years. Besides that, he was so far out of her league in many areas, but he never made her feel less than. He was down to earth and made her feel like the most important person in his world.

Genesis glanced at the bouquet.

Agreeing to date Noah had turned into the best decision she'd ever made. She was so in love with him, but her only concern was her past. A past that Noah only knew a little about.

One day she'd share everything, but for now, she was going to enjoy having him in her life.

Chapter Two

"Tonight was so much fun," Genesis said as she and Noah stepped into his house.

The two of them along with one of his brothers and his wife had gone to dinner and then ventured out to an escape room.

"It was an incredible experience, but I'm glad I didn't have to go it alone. Otherwise, I never would have gotten out of those rooms."

Noah chuckled as he helped her off with her wrap and draped it over a hanger in his mudroom. "I know, right? That last one had me stumped. Though I hate to admit it, had Ashton not been there, we probably would've run out of time," he said of his brother, who was a former Atlanta PD detective.

Ashton currently worked for Supreme Security—or as some referred to them, Atlanta's Finest—an organization that provided personal security to Atlanta's rich and famous. The escape room had a prison break theme, and he and Noah were amazing when it came to figuring out the clues. They all made it out with a minute to spare.

Genesis couldn't remember the last time she'd had that much fun, but the experience was definitely brain overload. Now all she wanted to do was curl up with Noah and get some sleep.

"Have I told you how much I love you?" Noah asked and backed her against the long, center island in his state-of-the-art kitchen. He boxed her in with both of his arms on each side of her and his palms resting on the counter.

The first time he professed his love to her had been a month into their relationship. Genesis would've thought it strange or uncomfortable had she not felt the same way. Noah had a reputation for being quick to make decisions and always getting what he wanted. Unlike her who usually overthought everything. Yet, in this case, they were of the same mind. Genesis never knew she believed in love at first sight, but then she met Noah.

Her heart melted as she stared into her man's alluring, dark amber eyes, and she smiled. "You might've mentioned it a few times, and I love you." Actually, she was *crazy* in love with this man, and that scared and excited her.

She'd had her share of crushes growing up and had even thought she was in love a time or two while in her twenties. But now at thirty-three and dating a strong, handsome, successful man who made her feel like the luckiest woman in the world, Genesis realized those other relationships were a prelude to what she and Noah shared. He meant the world to her, and joy danced inside of her whenever they were together.

Still smiling, she cupped his face and brushed the pads of her thumbs over the light stubble on his cheeks. Normally, he was clean-shaven, but he hadn't shaved in a few days, and she liked this look. This sexy, sophisticated, yet rugged look he was sporting.

His hands roamed down the side of her body and over the curve of her hips. "I think this sweater dress is my favorite outfit that I've ever seen on you."

The royal blue dress was comfortable and cute. It wasn't as thick as some sweater dresses, but it had been perfect for the cool evening.

"I especially like the buttons. Easy access," Noah said as he slowly undid the first one, and then the second one all the while peppering kisses against her lips and along her jawline.

His heady scent of sandalwood wrapped around her like a cashmere blanket, and Genesis moaned. She wanted to nestle against him and bury her nose in the crook of his neck, but the way he was kissing and touching her made her want way more than that.

Noah helped her out of the dress and laid it on the counter. That left Genesis in nothing but a baby-blue, satin bra and panty set along with three-inch heels. She shivered and it had nothing to do with the temperature but everything to do with the way Noah was looking at her.

As his heated gaze traveled the length of her, Genesis bit down on her bottom lip. She might not be skinny like the women she'd heard he usually dated, but there was nothing wrong with her self-confidence as it related to her body.

She embraced her curves, every single one of them, and she already knew that Noah didn't have any complaints. Like many Black men, he liked his woman with a little meat on her bones. He'd said as much, and what he didn't say in words, he said with his eyes.

He liked what he saw.

"You're so damn beautiful." The huskiness of his voice sparked the passion swirling inside of her. Especially when he lifted her into his arms and carried her to the family room. She wasn't sure why they didn't go upstairs to his bedroom, but that was okay. She wanted him, and it didn't matter where they made love.

Noah didn't stop moving until he reached the large leather sectional that took up much of the space in the room that sported twenty-foot ceilings. The furnishings gave the area a masculine feel. Yet, the modern, electric fireplace, family photos mounted on light-gray walls, and the thick gray carpet that covered the floor made the room feel cozy and inviting.

He placed her on the wide cushions, then stood back and started undressing himself.

Genesis watched his every move. First went his button-down shirt, then his T-shirt, and when his hands went for his belt buckle, she licked her lips without thinking.

The man's body was a work of art, and that included the omega symbol branded over his heart. She had traced the horseshoe-looking emblem with her tongue more than once, and the desire to do it now was almost overwhelming. Noah had gotten it after pledging Omega Psi Phi fraternity while in college, and it only added to his sexiness.

Her gaze took in his wide shoulders, his brawny biceps, and the way his sinewy muscles flexed as he undressed. Then there were his toned legs that seemed to go on forever. But what had her pulse amping was his dick—that had her complete attention. Long. Thick. Hard.

This was exactly what she needed tonight. Noah, his body, and all that he could do with it. The last few weeks had been stressful with one thing after another, but it was Ronnie's appearance in her life that troubled her.

Genesis ran into him again two days ago near the coffee shop that was doors away from her office building. He said he lived in the area, and that he grabbed coffee there every morning. Before recently, she had never seen him in the area.

Were the run-ins a coincidence? She didn't think so, especially since she didn't believe in coincidences.

Was Ronnie trying to work his way back into her life? Maybe. But if that was the case, they were going to have a problem. Though she wanted the best for him, she also wanted him as far away from her as possible. He was her past. A past that she had worked hard to move on from.

"What's wrong?" Noah asked as he pulled a condom from his wallet and dropped the foil packet on the coffee table. He lay down beside her. "You've been distracted a lot lately. Want to talk about it?"

Genesis ran her hand up his bare chest and smiled. "All I want to do right now is enjoy you."

She didn't want to talk. Nor did she want to think. All she wanted was to have him inside of her.

Noah turned and gently lowered her onto her back and made quick work of helping her out of her underwear. When he returned to her mouth, he nibbled on her top lip, then her lower one before slipping his tongue between her lips.

Oh yes. He was right where she wanted him, doing exactly what she needed him to do.

Genesis glided her hands up his torso and wrapped her arms around his neck and held him close as he deepened their connection. Ripples of pleasure charged through her veins as his kiss became more demanding.

She lifted her hips as he ground against her. He felt so good. So good that she wanted to feel more of him, wanted him to have his way with her, and wanted to forget about the past week. Her day-to-day work, the event planning, and Ronnie. She wanted to block it all out and enjoy this moment with the man she absolutely adored.

Noah moved his mouth from hers and trailed kisses down her neck, over her shoulders and he didn't stop until he reached her breasts. His hands and mouth on her body sent her temperature rising, and Genesis squirmed beneath him.

A moan pierced the air, and she wasn't sure if it was from him or her. It didn't matter. Nothing else mattered but right here and right now.

Her eyes drifted closed, and her nipples hardened as currents of desire shot to the tips of her toes while Noah worshiped her breasts. With such gentleness, he swirled his tongue around one sensitive nipple before capturing it in his mouth. Adrenaline pumped through her veins as he sucked and teased her hardened peak.

They might've only been dating for a few months, but this man knew how to work her body. Genesis whimpered with each lap of his tongue over her heated skin. Between his heady scent floating around her, and the way his hands caressed her body, the tantalizing throbbing at the apex of her thighs increased. Especially when he paid her other breast the same attention. With every flick of his tongue, her passion rose. She was so aroused that it felt as if she'd leap out of her skin.

When Noah lifted and started to move away, Genesis whimpered until she realized he was grabbing the condom. He made quick work of sheathing himself and positioned himself between her thighs.

He stared down into her upturned face, and the love radiating in his eyes had her heart melting. How'd she get this lucky? The man was what fantasies were made of from his powerful body to his sharp mind, and...

Ohhh, Genesis sucked in a breath when his heavy erection bumped against her wet opening before he slid into her.

"Ohh, yes," she purred as he moved inside of her, and she caught his rhythm. Her internal walls contracted around his dick as he went deeper, harder, and gradually picked up speed.

The erotic sounds he was making and the feel of him buried to the hilt had her passion rising. But when he slowed, her eyes popped open.

"How about we do your favorite position?" he asked, his breaths coming in short spurts.

No other words were needed. He moved from above her, giving her enough space to get on her hands and knees, then entered her from behind. Heat rippled under her skin as he drove into her and the sound of their heavy breathing and flesh slapping against flesh filled the quietness of the room.

"N—Noah," she panted and gripped the arm of the sofa as his powerful thrusts pushed her closer to her release, and... "Noah!" she cried out as currents of pleasure charged through her, gripping her body with such force she saw stars flitting before her eyes. "Ohhhh, my..."

Genesis gasped for air and would've collapsed against the sofa cushion, but Noah held her up around the waist. He continued driving into her until he reached his own release.

He lay heavily against her back, and they both collapsed to the cushion. Genesis sputtered a laugh, and Noah gave her a quick peck on the lips before he settled next to her. For the next few minutes, their chests heaved until they were finally breathing normally.

A wave of contentment settled over Genesis, and all thoughts of the last couple of weeks were placed way back inside her mind. She was in love with the most gentle, loving man who had stormed into her life and turned it around for the better.

"Be right back," Noah said. He gave her a quick peck on the lips and headed to the first-floor bathroom.

When he returned, he pulled her into his arms and covered them with the multi-color throw that was draped on the back of the sofa.

Genesis's head rested on his chest, and the song, "Never Knew Love Like This Before" by Stephanie Mills came to mind.

It was more than just the sex that had her basking in the afterglow of their lovemaking. It was everything. It was the way he made her feel, the way he touched her and looked at her. She always saw so much love and respect in his eyes, and the thought that his feelings for her were just as strong as hers were for him meant everything.

She tilted her head back and glanced up at Noah's handsome face. "You're amazing," she said.

"Funny, I was thinking something similar about you. You mean so much to me." He pushed a few braids away from her face and slid them behind her ear before slowly brushing the back of his fingers down her cheek.

His words were spoken with so much conviction that Genesis felt them to the depths of her soul.

He kissed her sweetly, then said, "Marry me."

Genesis's mouth fell open, and she blinked several times, sure that she hadn't heard him correctly. "Umm... what?" she croaked, then cleared her throat. "What did you say?"

"Marry me. This isn't how I planned to propose, but I couldn't wait. I love you, sweetheart, and I want to spend the rest of my life with you. Say that you'll be my wife."

Ohmigod. Ohmigod. Ohmigod.

Her brain went haywire as she struggled to process what he was asking.

Noah lifted slightly. She didn't know what he saw on her face, but whatever it was had him sitting up fully. Concern filled his eyes. "Genesis?"

"I—I—I can't," she sputtered, tears filling her eyes as her heart cracked open. "I... I can't marry you."

Chapter Three

"She said, no," Noah spat out and jabbed the punching bag harder.

I—I can't. I... I can't marry you, she'd said, and the words played on a loop inside of his head. It didn't make sense. They were in love and meant for each other. They had even talked about a future together.

"How the hell could she say no?" he growled as his breaths came in short spurts while he continued throwing punches.

Ashton, who was holding the bag, chuckled. "You had sex with her and then asked her to marry you. Even a bonehead like you should've been able to come up with a better proposal. Who does that? Screw her brains out, then pop the question. That's tacky, man. You would've had a better chance of her saying yes had you proposed to her while we were going through the escape room last night.

"I couldn't! I don't have a ring."

Ashton froze, then shook his head and released the bag. "Yo ass proposed and didn't even have a damn ring? Man, what's wrong with you? It's not like you don't have the money, and you knew you wanted her to be your wife. Why weren't you prepared?"

"Shit, Ash, it's not like I had planned to propose at that moment. The words just... they just popped out."

His heart had been so full, it felt like it was going to burst from his chest. Genesis was the first person he thought of when he opened his eyes every morning and the one he thought of when he laid his head down at night. She meant everything to him, and that feeling had been so overwhelming last night that he couldn't help but propose.

But now she was gone.

That's why Noah had called his brother first thing this morning. He needed to talk it out. They were currently in Noah's home gym, which contained everything found in a fully operational workout facility. From free weights to cardio equipment, and even a hundred-pound punching bag which he was currently pummeling.

He and Ashton, his youngest brother by two years, worked out together a few times a week. At just over six feet tall, they were close in height and had a similar athletic build. With both of them now in their early forties, they were serious about taking care of their bodies.

"You know I'm right," Ashton said when he returned to holding the huge bag that was hanging by a thick chain from the beam attached to the ceiling. "Last night probably wasn't the best time to propose."

He and Ashton didn't agree often, but this was one time Noah had to admit that his kid brother was right. Noah shouldn't have sprung a proposal on Genesis. He should've waited... planned the perfect proposal with the ring and all, but he hadn't.

He punched the bag harder, and his muscles screamed when he added a hook and uppercut combo. Boxing did more than keep him fit. It also helped clear his head. *Usually*. Yet, this morning, his brain was a jumbled mess.

"There's no doubt in my mind that she loves me," Noah said more to himself, but he was sure Ashton heard him, especially when the jerk started laughing.

"You always did have a high opinion of yourself. It's possible that she just wasn't that into you."

Instead of responding, Noah gave the bag one last punch that sent Ashton stumbling back a couple of feet.

Chuckling, his brother released the bag but turned serious. "Okay, I can admit that the two of you were crazy about each other."

"*Are*, asshole!" Noah barked. "We *are* crazy about each other, and I know she didn't want to say 'no.' Something stopped her from saying yes."

"Something like what?" Ashton asked, wiping his face with a towel that Noah had tossed to him. "Do you think the age gap has her concerned? Or could it be your money that's the problem?"

Both were valid questions. He and Genesis were at different stages in life in almost every area. Being older than her didn't bother him, but initially, it made her hesitant to date him. That, as well as the fact that he had money, and she worked at his firm. Still, all that and his millionaire status had become non-issues as they got to know each other.

"I don't know, man, but I honestly don't think it's anything like that. Something has her on edge, and I need to know what it is so I can help fix it."

Noah hadn't thought too much about her behavior lately, until last night. Not until she turned him down, then left his house without saying goodbye.

After his disaster of a proposal, he had gone to the master bathroom to shower. Genesis used the shower in the guest room. But when he finished up and went in search of her, she was gone.

At first, he'd been shocked, then disappointed, and by the end of the night, he'd been pissed. Seeing the note had been like taking a punch to the gut. She had left him.

And she didn't even say goodbye.

That had been so out of character, and Noah didn't know what to make of her actions. That was when he started thinking back over the last couple of weeks.

There had been little things that he'd noticed but blew off. Like when she tossed and turned at night. He had assumed that she was restless because of all the work she was doing on the Juneteenth event. Then there were those evenings when he'd caught her staring off into space with sadness in her eyes. Similar to what he had witnessed last night. He also recalled her drifting in and out of conversations.

"Something has been bothering her, and I don't think it has anything to do with her and me," Noah said and took a long drag from the bottle of water he pulled from the small refrigerator in the corner.

He and Genesis had been growing closer with each day that passed. They had even professed their love for each other. Besides that, there was no way she or her body would've responded to him the way it had if she didn't feel what he felt for her.

But why hadn't she confided in him? Surely, she had to know that there was nothing he wouldn't do for her. She was it for him. Which was why he wanted to spend the rest of his life with her.

Ashton leaned against the wall nearest the door. "Have you heard from her?"

"Not since last night. I texted to make sure she made it home safely. She responded, saying that she did and that she never meant to hurt me. But she had the nerve to add that we need a break from each other."

Noah hadn't responded because he had no intention of walking away. He'd give her a little space, but no way was he letting her walk out of his life without fighting for her... for them.

"I wish she would just talk to me and tell me what's going on."

"Do you think she's in some type of trouble?" Ashton asked.

"I don't know, but I have every intention of finding out."

Chapter Four

Genesis propped her elbows onto the kitchen table and covered her tired, red eyes. Last night had been one of the worst nights of her life, and this morning wasn't much better. It felt as if her heart had split open all over again. All she could think about was how she had walked out on Noah... the only man she had ever loved. He would never forgive her. Hell, she didn't think she would ever forgive herself.

Inside her head felt as if there was a jackhammer pounding against her skull. At least it was the weekend, and she didn't have to go to work. She was still dressed in her fluffy robe with her braids piled on top of her head with no intention of ever leaving the house again. Of course, that was wishful thinking, especially if Samantha Lewis, her best friend, and roommate, had anything to say about it.

It was eight in the morning and with only three hours of fitful sleep, Genesis wanted to go back to bed. She couldn't. Samantha was in the process of giving her a lecture.

Genesis reopened her eyes as her friend paced near the table, huffing out a frustrated breath every few minutes. When she finally stopped moving, she leaned on the back of a kitchen chair and her light brown eyes bore into Genesis.

She and Sam were average height for women, and they both had hourglass figures and reddish-brown skin. That's where the physical similarities stopped. Genesis wore her hair in micro-braids and had a girl-next-door vibe about her. Whereas Sam was adventurous and seemed to change her appearance every other week.

But right now, she looked like the girl Genesis had grown up with in foster care. Her natural hair with highlights was curly and shoulder length, and her beautiful face was scrubbed clean of makeup. She could've easily passed for a college student.

Unfortunately, she was wearing her badass investigator expression. That meant one thing; questions were coming. As far as Genesis was concerned, it was too early in the morning to be interrogated.

"Help me understand what you were thinking," Samantha said. "It doesn't make sense. You are crazy in love with that man—a man who worships the ground you walk on, I might add. Yet, Noah asked you to spend the rest of your life with him, but you said *no*. I don't get it."

"Sam, just let it go."

"I can't. I can't watch my bestie miss out on the love of her life. I have known you since you were a snot-nose kid standing on the porch of our last foster home. I have been with you for life's highs and lows. I know you, Gen, probably better than anyone in this world."

There was no doubt about it. Samantha knew her better than anyone, and sometimes that was a pain. Genesis had been fourteen when she arrived at the foster home where Sam and Ronnie lived. They had become her best friends... her family.

"You have never been as happy as you've been in the last few months, and I know a big part of that is because of Noah.

Honey, you have always dreamed of getting married and having a family, and Noah is offering that to you. I don't get..."

Genesis banged her fists on the table. "Just stop! Okay?" Anger and heartbreak warred within her. "It's done. Noah and I are finished! So, get over it!" Genesis yelled and jerked out of her chair, practically knocking it over in the process.

Unable to listen to any more, she stomped out of the kitchen and headed to her bedroom.

"Gen, wait." Samantha followed her to the back of the three-bedroom, two-and-a-half bath house that they were renting. "I'm sorry. I know you're hurting, and I hate that, but please just talk to me."

Genesis stormed into her room and fell back on the bed. She stared at the ceiling. "Noah doesn't know about my past," she said, barely loud enough for Samantha to hear. "He doesn't know about Ronnie, and he doesn't know that I almost... well, you know. I couldn't say *yes* to Noah's proposal when there are secrets between us."

"Oh, honey. Why didn't you just tell him everything?"

The mattress barely moved when Sam sat on the edge of it. Not because she was a lightweight, but because Noah had insisted on buying Genesis the best mattress that money could buy. He had claimed she needed something that could better accommodate them whenever he spent the night.

Tears pricked Genesis's eyes, but she didn't let them fall. She had cried so much the night before, that she was surprised that she had tears left.

"I have seen the two of you together, and there is no doubt that he adores you. There's nothing you could say or do that would change that. Do you trust him?"

Genesis glanced at her friend. "Of course, I do. I trust him with my life."

"Then tell him... *everything*," she insisted. "He's a good man, Gen. Don't let your past make you miss out on an amazing future."

"It's not that simple, Sam. I don't know what I was thinking when I started dating him in the first place. Noah is so out of my league, and he's often in the spotlight. Hell, he's Mr. Black Atlanta," she said.

Noah was a member of a national organization of Black men who supported and celebrated Black culture. They had chapters in most major cities, and every four years a Mr. Black representative was chosen for their chapter. Noah was in his last year as Mr. Black Atlanta.

"Do you know what it could do to his reputation if we married and the media... or even his family found out about my past? It's bad enough that I grew up in foster care, but if he found out about—"

"That's why you need to tell him. If it ever comes out, let it come from you."

Genesis was actually surprised that one of his brothers hadn't done a deep background check on her. Ashton used to be a detective, and he had another brother, Ian Chambers, who worked for the FBI.

Or maybe they had done a background check, and Noah just hadn't told her.

No. No way, she thought as soon as the idea popped into her mind. Noah knew she'd grown up in foster care. He also knew that she ended up in the system because her mother killed her father and then killed herself, leaving her as an orphan.

Nah, if he knew about what happened that night Ronnie was arrested, Noah would've said something.

Genesis wanted to tell him, but she didn't want him to think less of her. She didn't want him to look at her with pity or even disgust. Besides that, she'd have to explain Ronnie, and he was the last person that she wanted Noah to find out about.

"Ronnie called me again," she said to Sam, and her friend groaned.

"I hope you told him to find the nearest cliff and jump off it. I'm telling you, Gen, he's up to no good. I hate that you can't see that."

"Sam, if it weren't for Ronnie, I would've—"

"Don't give me that shit about him saving your life. Despite what you might think that bastard only cares about one thing—himself. The sooner you get him out of your life, the sooner you can focus on your future."

"Don't worry. I didn't talk to him." Genesis sat up and tightened the belt of her robe. "As a matter of fact, I blocked his number. Hopefully, he'll get the message."

She hadn't been thinking when she gave him her cell number during lunch that first day they ran into each other. She'd been glad to see him, and initially, it had been like catching up with an old friend. But by the time they'd finished eating lunch that day, Genesis had wished she hadn't exchanged numbers with him.

It wasn't that he had said anything inappropriate or even done anything wrong. It was a feeling. A feeling deep inside of her that made her wary where Ronnie was concerned.

"I've always thought he was a jerk," Samantha said. "I don't know how you never saw that."

Genesis hadn't seen it because Ronnie had always looked out for her. He was her big brother. It had been like that from the moment the social worker dropped her off at the house. She didn't know why, but he treated her like his little sister.

"From day one, he was nice to me," she said to Samantha.

If anyone stepped to her the wrong way at school, Ronnie was right there to protect her. He also gave her money. Whether it was for field trips, school supplies, or the latest gym shoes that she wanted, he came through for her when her foster mother couldn't... or wouldn't.

Ronnie had always been a hustler, picking up odd jobs even as a young teenager. Their foster mother wasn't as strict with him as she'd been with Genesis and Samantha. As long as he stayed out of trouble and got home at a reasonable time, that's all she cared about.

"I understand that you have some type of hero worship going on when it comes to Ronnie, but what about Noah?"

The mention of his name sent a wave of sadness crashing through Genesis. She wanted Noah in her life, but not until she got rid of Ronnie. Or she could do what Samantha said and tell Noah about what happened sixteen years ago.

Just the thought of having to do that made her breakout into a cold sweat. She couldn't tell him. At least not yet.

Samantha sighed loudly. "I don't trust Ronnie, and neither should you."

Now, Genesis was the one sighing. "Sam..."

"Don't let him be the reason you miss out on the best thing that ever happened to you," her friend continued. "He almost destroyed your life once. Don't let him get that chance again."

Chapter Five

Genesis reread the meeting notes that she had just typed up and groaned. "What is wrong with me?" she mumbled.

The meeting had been regarding one of their new campaigns for aerospace engineering, but her notes were all about Noah. His name showed up at least four times in three paragraphs, and he had nothing to do with the meeting.

Genesis growled under her breath and rested her forehead on the desk. She had barely made it through the last few days with her sanity. She had told Noah that they needed to take a break, and he had backed off. No calls. No flowers. Nothing. He gave her what she'd asked for, and Genesis hated it.

She missed him so much. Too many times she had picked up the phone to call him, but she hadn't. She couldn't. At least not yet. What she had to tell him could ruin everything they'd built, and she couldn't take that chance. Granted, she'd probably already destroyed any chance of them being together again, but...

I'll tell him. One day. I'll tell him everything.

Right now, she needed to get those notes typed up correctly and send them to her supervisor.

Genesis lifted her head and got back to work. She made the corrections and had just finished reading through the document when her desk phone rang.

"Hi, this is Genesis," she said, holding the receiver between her ear and shoulder. "May I help you?"

"Hey, Genesis, this is John. You have a call that came through the mainline. I'm going to patch it through."

"Thanks," she said absently and moved the phone to her other ear.

She quickly emailed the meeting notes to her supervisor. A second later, she heard someone say, "Hello" on the other end of the phone.

"Hi, this is Genesis. May I help you?" she asked and leaned back against her seat.

"What's up, Gen? I was hoping I'd catch you before you headed to lunch," the male voice said through the phone, and the hair on the back of Genesis's neck stood at attention.

No. No. No. It can't be.

"Hello? Hello? Gen, you there?"

"Yes," she whispered and sat forward. "How'd you know where I worked?"

Ronnie chuckled. "Come on, Gen. I ran into you twice near the same location, and last week I saw you walk into this building. The same building where I met with a realtor a few minutes ago. Anyway, I need to talk to you... in person."

"No. Ronnie, that's not a good idea. It was great running into you, but..." What could she say that wouldn't sound callous? Because what she really wanted to say was, *Lose my number.*

"Come on, Gen. I finally have some good news, and you're the first person I thought of to share it with. I'm getting ready to leave. Meet me downstairs in the parking structure."

"I started to come to your office. I thought better of it," Ronnie said, snatching her out of her thoughts. "But if you prefer, I can come upstairs instead of you coming down, then I—"

"I'll be there shortly," she hurried to say.

The last thing she wanted was for Ronnie to show up at her job. It was bad enough that he was in the parking structure. She needed to be firm and tell him that they couldn't be friends. Too much time had passed, and they were different people. He was a part of her past, and she needed to leave him there.

A short while later, Genesis took the elevator down to the main level of the parking structure. When the metal doors slid open, she stepped out and glanced around. She spotted Ronnie toward the end of the row. He was leaning against an old, black, four-door vehicle that had a huge dent near the back bumper. *Just be firm*, she told herself and headed in his direction.

He greeted her with a smile, and that guilt that always settled into her gut when it came to him returned.

"You get more beautiful every time I see you," he said as he pushed away from the car. He leaned in to hug her, but Genesis took a step back.

"Ronnie, it's not okay for you to come to my job like this or call me at work."

The smile slipped from his lips for a second but returned. "Not even to hear my good news?"

"What news?" she asked, wondering what was so important.

"Me and my buddy finished our business plan and we're moving forward and opening up a CBD and hemp dispensary. We've already been in contact with a bank. The loan officer said that at first glance, our paperwork looks good," Ronnie said with excitement.

"What about the body shop that you were planning to buy?" she asked, but then something else dawned on her. "Isn't CBD and hemp illegal here?" She wasn't sure, but Georgia was known for being more conservative than other states. "And as an ex-con, are you sure getting involved in the sale of any type of drugs is a good idea?"

"We'll be selling CBD, hemp oils, and other products like that. Don't worry, it's all above board," he said and clapped his hands while grinning. "I'm on my way, baby. I'm about to make a comeback! And I wanted my oldest friend to know."

Genesis wanted to ask more questions, especially since only weeks ago he was excited about buying a body shop. But this? She didn't know enough about CBD or hemp oils to ask any questions.

Actually, the more she listened to him, the more she didn't believe a word he was saying. Too much wasn't adding up. She recalled him mentioning stopping by the real estate office in her office building. Why did he need to work with an agent when he didn't have money? And there was no way a bank was loaning him anything. He had just gotten out of prison after spending all his adult life behind bars. He had no money, no credit, and he lived on his friend's sofa.

Nope. Not adding up.

Instead of saying any of that, she said, "Congratulations, Ronnie. I wish you well."

"Thanks. I knew you'd have my back. That's why I told my buddy that you might want to invest in our business. If not, if you can loan me ten G's, that would be great. I can repay you six months after we open."

Genesis looked at him as if he'd lost his mind. She never gave him the impression that she wanted any part of what he had planned.

"I'm not interested. Besides, I don't have that type of money, but I hope everything works out for you."

Ronnie chuckled. "Come on, Gen. You look like you're doing pretty well for yourself." He waved his hand up and down her body.

She glanced down at the yellow Chanel blouse that she had paired with off-white pants and high-heeled pumps to match. Yes, she tried to always dress nice, and she could admit to having a few designer pieces, but she didn't have that type of money to loan.

"Look, Ronnie. It's been nice seeing you again, but whatever you got going on, I'm not interested. As a matter of fact, don't call me anymore."

Her words came out harsher than she intended and by the sudden hardness of his glare, he didn't like what she'd said. But it was time she put an end to whatever nonsense he was up to.

"Yes, we were friends back in the day," she continued, "but that was a long time ago."

"Oh, excuse the hell out of me. I received good news and thought I'd share it with you. But I guess your ass is too good to be near the likes of me. Is that it?"

He moved closer, but she stood her ground, even when he got in her face. There was a hint of booze on his breath which he tried to mask with coffee, but it didn't work.

"Have you forgotten what I did for you? Have you forgotten the sacrifices I made... for you?"

Genesis gritted her teeth and balled her fists at her sides. Gone was the guilt that she'd been carrying around for years. In its place was anger. She could admit that he had come through for her more times than not, but she wasn't about to let him lay a guilt trip on her.

"Sacrifices?" she spat. "I appreciate the things you did for me when we were *kids*, but we're grown now. I know the score. Don't step to me talking about all you *sacrificed* for me. At least be honest with yourself. Most of what you did was for *you*, Ronnie, not me, and you know it."

Fire burned in his eyes, and his jaw ticked as he glared down at her, but Genesis refused to let him see her fear. Gone was the boy who looked after her, and she had no idea what this man was capable of. Yet, if she backed down, he'd keep coming around, and she couldn't have that.

As if a switch had turned on inside of him, his lips quirked, and a half smile kicked up the right corner of his mouth.

"I see you've grown a backbone," Ronnie said. "That's good, but your ass owes me, and I'm here to collect."

Chapter Six

This is a bad idea. A very bad idea, but Noah was going to do it anyway. He was going to Genesis and insist that she have lunch with him. It was past time they talked. *Really* talked.

Used to getting whatever he wanted, he refused to even entertain the idea of her saying no. Yet, it was a possibility. Genesis didn't do anything she didn't want to do. That was partly what drew him to her in the first place.

For years, especially after he made his first million, women threw themselves at him. It was either because they knew he had money, while other times it was because of his connections around the city. Genesis didn't care about any of that. As a matter of fact, because of those things, it had taken some effort to get her to go out with him. She had challenged him from day one, and he wouldn't have her any other way.

Damn, I miss her.

In the short amount of time that they'd been together, she had not only won his heart, but she was a huge part of his life. The last few days without her had been torturous, and he wanted her back.

The elevator doors slid open, and Carol gasped when she saw him.

"Oh, my goodness. I'm so glad I ran into you. Genesis might need you."

She pulled him onto the elevator, then pushed the button for the third floor. That was where her and Genesis's offices were located. Worry crept through his body and set him on edge, but Noah didn't want to jump to any conclusions.

"What happened? Is she okay?"

When the doors didn't close fast enough for her, Carol pushed the button several more times. "Come on. Come on," she mumbled before the doors finally slid closed. The woman was a bit eccentric on any given day, but this behavior was weird even for her.

"Carol, tell me what the hell—"

"You look really nice by the way," she said, eyeing his brown Henley and khakis. "Strong, powerful, and lethal. That's perfect. It'll help," she said more to herself than to him just as the elevator doors closed.

"Carol," he growled. "Where. Is. Genesis?"

"Okay. Okay. I just returned from a dentist appointment, and I saw her on the ground level of the parking structure."

Noah gritted his teeth. His patience was shot. "And?"

"She wasn't alone," Carol whispered, and Noah stiffened. She wouldn't be telling him this, whispering the words, if Genesis had been with a woman.

"Genesis was with a guy who doesn't look like someone she would hang out with. I've never seen him around here before."

The elevator stopped on the third floor, and before Carol could say more, the doors swooshed open. She stepped out just as two men stepped in, and Noah reached out to hold the doors open.

"Why did you tell me that?" he asked.

"Because I think you should go and check on her. *Now*."

Noah nodded, and a surge of unease charged through him as he pushed the button for the ground floor of the parking garage.

Who was the guy? Did he have anything to do with whatever was going on with Genesis? And what was it about him that put Carol on edge?

As the elevator stopped on two more floors to let off other passengers, Noah rubbed his hands together. More questions pinged around in his mind, but most importantly, he hoped Genesis was all right.

He stepped off the elevator and didn't see them right away, but raised voices caught his attention, and he followed the sound. That unease he had experienced moments ago grew into panic when all he heard was the traffic on the busy street beyond the walls of the garage.

Why'd they stop talking?

He kept moving, weaving around cars, and trying not to imagine the worst. Maybe Carol had been overreacting, but deep down, Noah didn't think so. The older woman had been genuinely concerned.

"I'm not doing this with you." Noah heard Genesis say just before he spotted her and a guy at the back of the lot in a heated discussion.

Noah took in the man. Baseball cap pulled low over his eyes. Dark blue T-shirt and rugged jeans with an oil stain on the front left thigh. Dusty black workboots covered his feet.

The guy didn't look familiar, and Genesis was holding her own. For a split second, Noah debated on whether to approach, but then the man grabbed Genesis's arm.

Noah's feet started moving in their direction before he realized it, but some sane part of him insisted that he slow down. The last thing he wanted to do was make this situation worse than it might've been. He needed to keep his head and come up with something quickly.

"There you are," he said, struggling like hell to keep his voice calm even though the man released her. "You ready for lunch?"

Would she play along or was he going to have to think of something else to get her away from the guy? And yes, he definitely wanted her away from him, because the wariness in her eyes put Noah on edge.

Genesis was the sweetest, most easy-going woman he knew. Right now, though, her body was stiff, and she had a death grip on the small purse in her hand.

"Yes, I'm ready." She started to move toward Noah, but the guy grabbed her arm again.

Noah lunged forward. One minute he was about to reach for Genesis's hand, and the next, he had his hands wrapped around her visitor's neck. He slammed the guy against the trunk of a four-door sedan and leaned over him.

Genesis gasped. "Oh, my God. Noah, please. Don't do this. Let's... let's just go."

"Don't you ever put your hands on her again." Noah almost didn't recognize his own voice that held so much venom. It was no wonder the punk was looking at him with wide eyes. "I don't know who you are, and I don't care. Just stay the hell away from her."

The man had his arms up and out in surrender, but Noah wasn't buying it. This guy reeked of trouble, and there was no fear in his eyes, which, in Noah's opinion, made him a very dangerous man.

"Genesis is my sister," the man said. "I would never hurt her. So, you can back the hell up off me."

Brother? She has a brother?

"Noah, come on," Genesis said and tugged on his arm. "Let's go."

Noah didn't want to let go of the asshole. He wanted to beat the crap out of him on principle alone. Twenty years ago, he probably would've, but now... Now he had too much to lose and too many people counting on him to keep his head in situations like this. Besides, he needed answers, and the only person he wanted the responses to come from was Genesis.

Noah gave the man's throat a squeeze before jerking him away. Then he turned to Genesis. "Let's get out of here."

With his fingers interlocked with hers as he led her away, it didn't go unnoticed that she didn't say anything else to her *brother*. No goodbye. No see you later. Nothing.

Exactly who was this guy really? Because Genesis was an only child.

TWENTY MINUTES.

It had been twenty minutes since she and Noah had arrived at her favorite Thai restaurant, and her nerves were tied in knots. What made it worse—the deafening silence vibrating between her and Noah.

Genesis knew the lack of conversation was on her. He was waiting for her to tell him what the hell he had walked in on in that garage.

She had expected him to question her the moment he had settled her into his two-seater Maserati. He hadn't. Besides asking her if she was all right, he hadn't asked about Ronnie, why they were in the garage, or what they'd been discussing.

To say that she'd been shocked when he showed up looking like a wet dream strolling through the parking garage would be an understatement. The man was gorgeous on any given day, but today, he somehow managed to look even hotter. He also looked like the wealthy millionaire that he was, which made her uncomfortable where Ronnie was concerned.

The server arrived with their meals and after making sure they had everything they needed, turned and left. Genesis's pad thai looked delicious, but she couldn't eat. So many emotions warred inside of her: shame, guilt, disappointment, joy, and even happiness, but Genesis couldn't seem to settle on one.

But one thing was for sure, she couldn't think of any other place she'd rather be than there with Noah. Her gaze met his just as he lifted a glass of scotch to his tempting lips. He sipped the dark liquid as his eyes searched hers.

Damn, the man was fine. He looked absolutely lickable, and it was taking all her restraint not to move to the other side of the table and crawl into his lap.

That thought alone let her know that she wasn't thinking straight. Not the part about him looking lickable because he did, but the part where she straddled him. She couldn't help it. She wanted to forget the last forty minutes, and Noah had the ability to give her that.

Not going to happen. Genesis knew him well enough to know nothing would ever happen between them again until he got answers.

She picked at her food. "I don't know what to say."

"What do you mean?"

Her gaze shot to Noah's, and she straightened in her chair. "Huh?"

He frowned at her and lowered his glass to the table. "You just said, *'I don't know what to say,'* and I said, 'What do you mean?'"

Crap. I said that out loud?

She propped her elbows on the table and held her head in her hands. Time's up. She needed to come clean, but not here. Not with people sitting all around them. Still, Genesis had to give him something.

She glanced up. "His name is Ronnie Peterson, and he's my foster brother."

Seconds ticked by as they stared at each other. For a minute, she didn't think he would respond, but then he asked, "Are you involved with him?"

Genesis startled at the question, and it felt as if she'd been slapped. "No!" she said emphatically and reached across the table, covering his hand with hers. "Noah, I am *definitely* not involved with him in any way. You have to believe me. I would *never* cheat on you. I love you." *And I always will.*

She kept that last part to herself, but she needed him to know that there was no one else.

"You're the only man for me."

Noah turned his hand over, and her smaller hand settled within his grasp. "Then why did you say no to my proposal?"

"Because..."

"Because?"

"Because I need to take care of something from my past before you and I can move forward."

A frown marred his handsome face. "Something like what? Does it have anything to do with Ronnie?"

"Yes."

Noah stood and moved to the seat next to her. He was still holding one of her hands, and his other arm was around her back. He leaned in close. "Are you in some type of trouble? Because if you are, I can—"

"No, baby. I'm not in trouble." Genesis eased her hand from his grasp and slipped it behind his neck. She pulled him to her and had only planned to give him a quick peck, but Noah had other ideas.

He cupped her face between his hands and his sweet, demanding lips caressed hers.

Genesis missed him so much, and the love she felt for this man was almost suffocating. She hated how she had botched things up the other day. But if his kiss was any indication, he forgave her. He ravished her mouth, as if they'd been apart for years instead of days, and Genesis was here for it. Except they still had unfinished business.

As if sensing her thoughts, Noah eased his mouth from hers, but his hands stayed on her face. "I love you so much, but we will never be able to move forward if I don't know what's going on."

Genesis eased out of his hold. When she glanced around, a few people were looking at them.

"I'm sorry... for everything," she said quietly. "I didn't mean to hurt you, and I hate the way I left the other day. I just... you caught me off guard, and I panicked."

The one thing Genesis had wanted to prevent was Noah knowing that Ronnie existed. Maybe she was being unreasonable... or naive... or just a wimp. Either way, she didn't want her foster brother anywhere near Noah, especially now.

At first, she hadn't wanted their paths to cross because she didn't want any questions about Ronnie's time in prison. It was one thing for Noah to know she grew up in foster care. It was another for him to know that she had been with Ronnie the night of his arrest.

There had never been more than a friendship... a brother/sister relationship between her and Ronnie. But if... No not if, when she went into details about her foster brother, Noah might think there was more between them.

One question would lead to others, and she had no idea how he would respond or react. Yet, Genesis had to trust his love for her. She had to believe that he loved her completely, no matter what.

"I have appointments for the rest of the afternoon, but how about tonight we—"

"I can't tonight," Genesis interrupted and ran her hand down his hard chest. "I have a committee meeting this evening, but if you're free tomorrow night, I'll cook dinner for us."

"Why can't we hook up after your meeting?" he asked, searching her eyes as if trying to figure out what she was hiding.

"Because," Genesis swallowed, "tomorrow night would be better. We can talk over dinner, and I'll answer any questions you have."

Chapter Seven

The next day, Noah was just finishing up an email when the alarm on his cell phone blared, and he shut it off. He was working from home and had fifteen minutes before he had to hop on a Zoom call with some friends.

But what he really wanted to do was hear Genesis's voice. Sure, he had talked with her the night before, and again this morning, but it wasn't enough. He wanted to go back to what they had—where he saw her daily and they spent most nights together.

Soon he'll know everything. He just hoped that whatever she was working through wouldn't come between them. But the fact was, she had said no to his proposal and Ronnie had something to do with it. Suddenly, all types of red flags were waving in front of him.

Don't go there, man. Trust your woman.

Genesis was the one he wanted to spend the rest of his life with. Whatever she was going through, they'd figure it out.

Noah glanced at the clock on his computer and stood. Knowing that he and the guys would probably talk for an hour, he headed to his kitchen for another cup of coffee.

He was looking forward to talking with the fellas—The Three Wisemen. He smiled at the name. He was actually one of the three, and all of them were members of Mr. Black, a national organization of Black men who supported and celebrated Black culture around the country.

He had first met Caspian Yearwood, who lived in Charlotte, and Jared Desdune who was out of Miami, at the annual Mr. Black networking event—Bold. Loyal. Ambitious. Cool. King. That had been seven years ago, and the three of them had been tight ever since.

Over the years, they hung out together when attending various Mr. Black events, and someone in the organization had dubbed them The Three Wisemen. The name fit them perfectly. Noah considered them all sharp, successful, and together they knew something about everything.

By the time he returned to his office, Caspian had logged on to Zoom.

"What's up, man?" Noah said and set his coffee mug on the desk as he reclaimed his seat. "How's everything? I see Jared is late. He probably took a break to play a video game."

Caspian chuckled, the hearty sound booming through the computer speakers. "Yeah, that brother might be serious about running The Carrington Resort in Biscayne Bay, but it wouldn't surprise me if he has a gaming console in his office."

Noah grinned at the truth in that statement. The five-star luxury resort Jared managed took up a lot of his time, but he knew how to sit back and chill too.

"I'm going to have to get some pointers from him on how to balance a workday. Actually, I don't know how either of you do it. I feel like all the balls I'm juggling these days are falling all over the place."

Caspian shook his head, and Noah noted how tired his friend looked. The former college football star was over ten years younger than Noah, but the guy had accomplished a lot in his thirty-one years. Caspian was the youngest of the three of them but seemed to have his life on the right track. He owned a successful company that created innovative business solutions for other organizations. Not only that, he oversaw numerous community initiatives, while also having a wife.

Before Noah could question him, Jared joined the call.

"What's going on, my brothers?" Jared said. The guy was dressed to impress in the dark three-piece suit he was wearing. He always looked as if he was heading to a photo shoot.

"All is well on this end," Noah said, though the moment the words were out of his mouth, his situation with Genesis popped into his mind, but he shook it free. "What's going on with you two? Oh, wait, congratulations, Mr. Black Charlotte," he said to Caspian. "I'm proud of you man, and I have no doubt that you're going to represent the organization well."

The organization had chapters in every major city, and every four years a new Mr. Black representative was chosen. While this would be Caspian's first year, Noah was in his last year, and Jared was in his second.

For the next few minutes, they talked Mr. Black business. The organization sponsored each community's Juneteenth celebration, but Mr. Black of each city was responsible for hosting the event.

Noah usually hosted a black-tie gala and silent auction the Saturday before Juneteenth. In Atlanta, that holiday was always filled with parades, fairs, comedy festivals, and other daytime events. So, he did it big with an evening of elegance that shined the spotlight on those making a difference in the Black community. Their plans this year were bigger and better than years before.

"This will be my first time hosting," Caspian said, explaining how he had an arts festival planned. It was a great idea, especially since his wife, Nia, did pottery, and it would give her an opportunity to showcase her work.

"What about you, Jared? What do you have planned for this year?" Noah asked.

"Since this is my first year as the manager of The Carrington Hotel, it's where I'm planning to have my event. I'll be bringing my A-game. We're going to have a Juneteenth Black Art Exhibition and Masquerade Ball."

As he talked, Noah could hear the determination in his voice. Jared not only wanted to spotlight the Mr. Black organization and Juneteenth, but he also wanted to show the owner of Carrington Hotels & Resorts that he had made the right decision in promoting him to manage one of his signature venues.

"By the way, do you guys remember Desirae?" Jared asked, changing the subject.

"Yeah, that's the woman who dumped you when you told her you wanted to see other women," Caspian said, shaking his head.

"Dude, it wasn't like that," Jared argued weakly.

It might not have been exactly like that, but Noah remembered that his friend had let the best thing that ever happened to him walk out of his life. All it would have taken was for him to be honest with her about his feelings. But no, instead of him telling her he wasn't interested in seeing other women, he let her believe the worst.

"Okay, okay, maybe that wasn't exactly like I remember," Caspian finally conceded, though he wasn't wrong, "but what about her?"

"She's one of the event designers interviewing to oversee the Juneteenth project."

"Ahh, hell," Noah said louder than intended. "Please tell me you're not the one who will be doing the interviews."

Jared sighed. "I wish I could tell you that, but there is no way I'm letting anyone else on staff interview her. Besides..." he started but stopped as if debating on saying more, and then he said, "I want another chance with her."

Wow. Noah hadn't expected that. He listened while Jared explained himself, and all Noah could do was wish him well with pursuing Desirae.

Caspian had gone quiet, and Noah didn't miss the way he rubbed his full beard, a sure sign something was bothering him.

"All right, Caspian, what's going on with you?" Jared asked before Noah could form the words.

Noah lifted his mug to his lips. The coffee had cooled but was now at the perfect temperature. "Before you say it's nothing," he piped in, "remember, we know you, and the way you're rubbing your beard says that something is heavy on your mind."

Caspian chuckled, then sighed. "It's Nia."

"Is she all right?" Noah asked concerned.

"Physically, she's fine, but she's pissed at me right now. Pissed enough to divorce me if I don't make some changes." Caspian ran a hand down his face, then rubbed the back of his neck.

"Okay, this sounds serious," Jared said.

"She's been complaining about all the time I spend here at the office and about the work I've been doing with the various community initiatives. Now that I'm Mr. Black Charlotte, she's livid. She thinks it'll be just one more thing that eats up my time. Time we should be spending together."

Noah listened as his friend shared his concerns about his marriage. Looking in from the outside, Noah thought Caspian had the perfect marriage. He and Nia came across as the "it" young, power couple who had it going on. Though that might still be the case, apparently, that didn't come without some conflict.

"Man, that's tough," Jared said and proceeded to give his opinion on what Caspian needed to do.

"Jared is right. You have to get your priorities in check," Noah said. "Though I'm not married, I have enough married folks in my life to know—your wife comes first. Always. All this other stuff you have going on might be important, but nothing should be more important than Nia."

"I know you guys are right, but—"

"Remember," Noah interrupted, "happy wife, happy life."

"Yeah, she means everything to me, and right now my baby ain't happy," Caspian said and was back to rubbing his beard again.

Noah hoped his friend could come up with a way to show Nia how much she meant to him. If anyone could do it, it was Caspian.

They talked a few more minutes until Caspian said, "Okay, enough about me. We know what's up with Jared, but what's going on with you, Noah? Are you still dating Genesis?"

Noah sighed loudly. He should've known he'd be next, but he didn't want to discuss his and Genesis's situation.

"Hmm... I guess there's trouble in paradise," Jared joked. "You might as well tell us what's up because even if I have another meeting in a few minutes, we're not getting off this call until you talk."

"So, talk," Caspian added, and Noah laughed.

"Fine. I asked Genesis to marry me."

"*Whaaat*? Ahh, man. That's great!"

"Dude! Congratulations!"

They both spoke at once, and their well wishes and excitement were like taking a punch to the gut. Noah didn't fail at much but having his marriage proposal turned down felt like just that. A failure.

"She said no."

Jared let out a curse. Noah didn't want their sympathy. Yet, he was in new territory. His brother Ashton had been right in saying that he hadn't had enough rejection to know how to deal with it. Noah could honestly say this was a first for him.

He filled the guys in on the botched proposal and how Genesis had asked for a little space.

"I have no doubt in my mind that she loves me as much as I love her, but there's something else at play here. Something to do with her past."

"Do you think it's another man?" Caspian asked, and Noah tensed as he thought about his encounter with Ronnie.

Genesis would never cheat on him, but there was something between her and her foster brother. Noah just didn't know what. Still, he said, "It's not another man."

"If she's been distracted, what made you propose that night? You said you hadn't planned to pop the question right then. Yet, you did anyway. Why?" Jared asked.

It was a good question that Noah had asked himself a dozen times.

"Because I'm crazy in love with the woman, and I don't want to live another day without her as my wife."

Chapter Eight

"Hold on a second, Kay," Genesis said into her cell phone.

She was in the grocery store picking up a few items for dinner. Standing in the middle of the bread aisle, she pushed her cart off to the side and pulled her earbuds from the side pocket of her crossbody bag.

"Okay, sorry about that," she said, adjusting the buds in her ear. "Now what were you saying?"

This was the second call she had received regarding the Juneteenth event. Though she and Carol had done most of the groundwork, they had a committee, as well as a virtual assistant, Kay, to help with some of the smaller details.

"You mentioned that the committee wanted to have a flag on the programs," the VA said, "but which one do you want to use—the Pan-African flag or the actual Juneteenth flag?"

"Hmm, that's a good question."

The red, black, and green Pan-African flag symbolized Black liberation in the United States. Genesis was leaning towards using that one because its colors were well-known in the Black community. Red was for the bloodshed and the struggle and sacrifice. While black represented the Black people, and green stood for the wealth of the land.

But in the late nineties, Ben Haith, the founder of the National Juneteenth Celebration Foundation, had created a flag to symbolize Juneteenth. The colors: red, white, and blue, were meant to demonstrate that even while enslaved, African Americans were American.

Genesis sighed. She had too many thoughts running through her mind to make the decision on the fly.

"Kay, that's a great question, but let me get back to you Monday. I want to run this by a couple of people before we decide."

They talked for a few minutes longer before disconnecting. Instead of returning her phone to her bag, Genesis shot off a quick text to Noah. Dinner was going to be a little late. She typed that she would call him when she left the grocery store. He didn't know it yet, but he was going to be on sous-chef duty.

A half hour later, Genesis hurried to her car. She loved that it was staying light out longer, but the sun had slid behind the horizon, and the sky was tinted with streaks of orange, yellow, and red.

Beautiful, she thought as she unlocked her car and placed the bags in the back seat before slamming the door.

"Hello, sweet Genesis."

Genesis screamed and whirled around with her hand on her chest. "Ronnie! Oh, my God! You scared me to death. What's wrong with you? What are you doing lurking around out here? And how did you even know I was here?"

"I have my ways." A smarmy smile spread across his face, and he moved closer.

His eyes were red, and he was twitching. That was something she hadn't noticed the other day. Was he high?

"I wanted to see you. We need to talk."

Her heart rate picked up speed. She glanced around trying not to look like she was checking out her surroundings. The parking lot was well-lit, but she didn't see anyone.

"I said all I had to say yesterday," she said, keeping her attention on him while taking small steps back. "I don't have that type of money to loan you, and even if I did, I wouldn't give it to you. The business sounds shady."

The smile that had been there moments ago disappeared, and a scowl marred his handsome face. "Don't give me that shit. I know you have money." He nodded his head toward her Honda. "Nice car. A cute little house in Buckhead that you share with Sam, and..."

Icy fear twisted inside her gut. She put more distance between them. He knew that she and Samantha were roommates, but Genesis never told him where she lived.

"Look at you," he said and waved his hand up and down at her. "Designer purse, nice clothes, and shoes that probably cost more than I make in a month. Don't tell me you can't loan me the money for my business."

The person she was looking at right now was not the boy who protected her... who once saved her life. What happened to that guy? What happened to her big brother?

"Listen, Ronnie. I don't have—"

"No, you listen!" he ground out.

His anger was palpable as he stepped toward her. Genesis shuffled back and bumped into a parked SUV.

"I need that money, and you're going to give it to me. If you don't have it, get it from that rich boyfriend of yours."

Genesis didn't respond and eased along the vehicle, trying to give herself enough room to run.

"You and Noah Chambers. Who would've thought? I looked him up. Not bad. Seems you've done *very* well for yourself while I had to rot in that hell hole, and it's all your fault! You owe me," he growled, sounding like a vicious dog.

Anger sparked inside of Genesis. "I don't owe you a damn thing! I didn't tell you to rob that store or pull a gun on that guy. That was all you!"

Ronnie backhanded her before Genesis saw the hit coming, and she screamed. Pain like nothing she had ever experienced exploded through her face. Her legs gave out, and she crashed to the ground. He punched her again before she could get her bearings.

"I'm done screwing around with you. You either get me the money, or you will regret the day you ever met me." He punctuated his words with a kick to her side, and she cried out as she curled into a ball, trying to catch her breath.

When he started to kick her again, Genesis grabbed his foot and tugged as hard as she could. That sent him stumbling back. The distraction gave her enough time to dig into her purse.

Just as he was about to charge at her again, she pulled the Ruger Max-9 from her purse and aimed it at him.

"Come any closer, and I will load your ass with lead," she said through gritted teeth while trying to keep them from chattering.

Her hands were steady, thanks to spending plenty of time at the gun range. But every nerve in her body was on edge, and her face was on fire as the jackhammer in her head pounded against her skull.

An arrogant smile spread across Ronnie's face. "You wouldn't shoot me."

"Try me," she said without hesitation and with enough steel in her voice to give him pause.

He narrowed his eyes. "After all that I've done for you, this is what it has come to?" He seemed to be sobering right before her eyes, and he inched closer.

"Stop!" she screamed. "Get away from me! Get away from me!"

"Hey! What's going on over there?" A deep voice came from somewhere behind her.

"Help me!" she screamed over and over again.

"Stupid, bitch! This ain't over," Ronnie ground out and took off in a sprint.

Genesis fumbled with her gun but managed to slip it back into her purse before a tall, thin man appeared.

"Hey. Are you all right?" he said and started toward her but suddenly stopped.

She wasn't sure what he saw on her face, but whatever it was had him looking uncomfortable. While he glanced around, Genesis struggled to stand and gritted her teeth when the pain in her side had her doubling over. She bit down on her bottom lip to keep from crying out. Her body pulsed with pain so intense that it stole her breath.

"Let me call 911 to get you some help."

"No!" Genesis said with more force than intended and dug deep for the strength to make it the few feet to her car. "I'm fine. If you can just open my car door, that's all I need." She pointed at the black Accord.

"I don't know, ma'am. You don't look steady on your feet. Please let me call someone to help you. Actually, there's a woman walking to her car in the next aisle. I'll get her attention and maybe she can—"

"No, I'm fine," Genesis said again, and swiped away a rogue tear, praying that more wouldn't fall before she could get rid of the good Samaritan. "Just open the car door. Please. That's all I need."

He mumbled something under his breath, but he did as she asked and stepped back.

"Thank you," she said as she eased into the car. The pain in her face and in her side was almost too much.

It wasn't until she closed her car door and waved at the guy did he finally walk away. The moment he did, Genesis burst into tears. She laid her head on the steering wheel and cried. She cried because of the pain. She cried because of Ronnie's betrayal, and she cried because of the friend... the brother that she had lost.

Genesis didn't know how long she stayed like that, but she knew she couldn't drive. Exhaustion had her barely able to keep her eyes open. Then there was the pain.

She had to call someone, and there was only one person that came to mind.

Chapter Nine

Tonight hadn't come fast enough. Since having lunch with Genesis yesterday, Noah had been counting the hours until he'd see her again. He half expected her to call and cancel, but so far, dinner was still on. He was less than a mile from her house, and soon he'd finally get to hold her close and get some answers.

His cell phone rang, and Noah smiled when Genesis's name popped up on the dashboard of his Range Rover. He answered with Bluetooth.

"Hey, sweetheart, are you just leaving the store? I'm almost at—"

"N—Noah... I—I need help," Genesis said, her voice raspy and barely a whisper.

Unease crept through him, and he gripped the steering wheel tighter as all his protective instincts kicked into gear. "What's going on? Where are you?"

"He... he hurt me," she sobbed, and dread rioted inside of Noah as he exited the highway.

"Gen—"

"Ron—Ronnie," she sputtered between sniffles. "P—please come get me. No police."

No police? What the hell?

Panic and fear battled within him. "Gen, where are you?" he demanded, unable to keep the anxiousness out of his voice.

Despite her sobs, he managed to figure out where she was in the parking lot of the grocery store. Promising to be there shortly, he disconnected that call and immediately called Ashton.

"Hey, what's up?" his brother's voice boomed through the speakers.

"Gen is in trouble, and I need some backup." He recounted the little that he knew and Genesis's location. "The grocery store is not too far from Supreme Security. Can you or one of the guys meet me? I'm not sure what I'm walking into."

"Yeah, me and Laz will head that way," Ashton said of his best friend, Lazarus Dimas.

They were once partners while they worked for Atlanta PD. Now they were personal security specialists with Supreme Security, also known as Atlanta's Finest. Many of them, like Ashton and Lazarus, were former law enforcement. While others were former military.

The whole team was badass, and Noah wouldn't mind having either of them by his side.

A few minutes later, he pulled into the parking lot looking for Genesis's Honda. It was a good thing she always parked away from the store to get in as many steps as she could. Otherwise, he didn't know how he'd find the car. The lot wasn't packed, but there were still enough vehicles parked that could've made finding her difficult.

Anxiousness rioted inside of Noah as he pulled in beside her car and jumped out. Just as he was heading to the driver's side, a big, black SUV with dark-tinted windows jerked into the parking spot on the other side of her.

Laz stepped out of the driver's side and Ashton out of the passenger side.

When Noah looked through the driver's side window of the Accord, fear lodged in his chest. Genesis was slumped over the steering wheel unmoving. He jiggled the door handle, then knocked on the window.

"Genesis!"

Her head shot up, and Noah jumped back from the door with his hands up.

What the hell?

"Shit." Came from either Laz or Ashton. Laz was on the other side of the vehicle, and Ashton was near the rear, peering in.

"Genesis, sweetie, it's me," Noah said and didn't take his eyes off the gun that she had pointed at him. "It's me."

"You didn't say anything about her carrying," Ashton said under his breath.

That's because I didn't know she owned a gun. How had he not known, and what the hell else didn't he know about her?

Genesis lowered the weapon, then burst into tears. Noah heard the doors unlock, but she made no move to open the door or exit the car.

"Go ahead. She put the gun on the passenger seat," Laz said, and he and Noah opened the car doors at the same time. Laz grabbed the gun before closing his door and stepping back.

Genesis's loud sobs gutted Noah. He felt helpless. "Aww, baby, don't cry. Where are you hurt?" he asked, afraid to touch her but needing to.

Her hands covered her face, and she was leaning awkwardly toward the center console.

"Gen..." Noah started, but gasped when she lowered her hands, and he got a clear view of her face. His heart stopped. "What the fuck?" he roared. "Ronnie did this to you? Ronnie? He's a dead man!"

Anger and shock rocked Noah to his core at the sight of his baby's swollen face. He couldn't move. He could barely think straight as fury clawed through him. He wanted to punch something or someone.

He wasn't sure how long he stood there stunned. It wasn't until Ashton said, "Move and breathe," did he snap out of his fog.

Ashton shoved him aside to get to Genesis.

Feeling like a total jerk, Noah turned away and ran his hand over his head and down to the back of his neck. Even after several deep breaths, he struggled to get air into his lungs.

Get it together, he told himself and heard his brother ask Genesis about her injuries.

"Sit tight. Be right back," Ashton said.

Seconds later he was tugging on Noah's arm and moving him a few feet away from the car.

"I'm going to kill him," Noah growled, and suddenly choked up, he bit down on his fist while gripping his brother's shoulder.

"You gotta keep it together—for her—she's going to need you," Ashton said under his breath and slapped a hand against Noah's chest. "She said this Ronnie guy punched her in the face and kicked her in the side. I can't tell if her ribs are cracked, but her left side is bruised. Unfortunately, she doesn't want to go to the hospital."

"Why the hell not? Oh, no. She's going," Noah started for her car, but Ashton stopped him.

"She doesn't want to report this asshole to the authorities, and if she goes to emergency looking like she does, there will be questions."

Noah was struggling to keep his anger under control. This couldn't be happening. "I should've beat that bastard's ass when I had a chance," he mumbled.

"I'm glad you didn't," Ashton said. "Otherwise, this situation could be worse."

Noah started toward her car. "Well, I'm ready to get her out of here."

Genesis was still sitting in the driver's seat, leaning against the headrest with her eyes closed and tears trickling down her swollen cheek.

She opened her eyes but didn't look at him. "I'm sorry for bringing this drama into your life," she murmured.

"Oh, baby," Noah said and placed a light kiss on her lips. Seeing her like this was killing him. "You have nothing to be sorry about. Give me a minute. I'm going to get you out of here and cleaned up."

Laz had disappeared for a few minutes and was walking toward them. Ashton filled him in, and Laz said something about hunting the motherfucker down.

As a former detective, if anyone could find Ronnie, it would be him and Ashton. Back in the day, they'd had that good cop/bad cop thing going, but in this case, Noah wanted the bad cop. No offense to his brother, but that would be Laz. The man skated on the line between right and wrong, and he always got his man.

"Let's take Genesis to see Angelo's brother, Dr. Mateo," Ashton said to Noah while Laz nodded. Angelo was also a security specialist with Supreme Security.

"I'm going to need some information about this Ronnie dude. Then I'll reach out to some of my contacts," Laz whispered as he glanced around.

Contacts meant some of his old confidential informants who he used to use when on the police force.

Noah huffed out a breath while rubbing the back of his neck where tension had built. "I appreciate whatever you guys can do. I want that asshole found as soon as possible. I don't care what it costs. I'll pay. Just find him 'cause his ass is mine."

Chapter Ten

Hours later, Noah carried a sleeping Genesis up to his bedroom. The doctor had given her pain medication, and she didn't stir. Not even when Noah removed her clothes and dressed her in one of his T-shirts.

Once she was tucked into bed, he stood over her and released a weary sigh. Relief had flooded through his body when they learned Genesis had no broken bones. Her bruises would take time to heal, and Noah had a feeling that wasn't all that would need healing. Being attacked by her foster brother, someone who claimed to be her friend, had to hurt in more ways than one.

Noah still didn't fully understand why Genesis refused to report the assault. She was okay with them hunting Ronnie down, but she insisted no cops.

Noah rubbed his tired eyes. After leaving the clinic, he, Genesis, Ashton, and Laz had gone to Genesis and Samantha's home. Since Sam was out of town for the next couple of weeks for work, Noah had insisted that Genesis stay with him. He half expected her to argue, but she didn't. If anything, she had looked relieved, and that told him that she was scared.

Ashton and Laz stayed with them the entire time. While Genesis had packed a few things that she would need, the guys had checked the interior and exterior of her home. Though

Genesis had a security system, there were no exterior cameras. That would be taken care of by tomorrow morning.

Now all they had to do was find Ronnie.

In the meantime, Noah planned to nurse Genesis back to health and get some answers.

GENESIS WINCED AND laid her hand on her bruised side as she readjusted the pillow behind her. Her face still throbbed, but at least it looked worse than it felt. That was thanks to Noah who had insisted on her keeping ice on her cheek every few minutes. She was pretty sure he'd kept the process going even after she had fallen asleep.

Leaning against the headboard, Genesis glanced at Noah's side of the king-size bed and her heart squeezed. He had lain beside her, but he'd been fully clothed in a T-shirt and pajama bottoms, then slept on top of the covers.

Normally, they slept in the nude, but not last night. Not because she'd been injured. It had everything to do with the fact that they weren't technically together anymore. And it was all her fault. She was the one who had wanted a little space. All because she feared he'd find out about her past before she was ready to share it.

I am such a fool.

She'd been calling herself all types of a fool since sitting in her car last night waiting for Noah to find her. Why had she even welcomed Ronnie back into her life? Well, she didn't actually let him back in. He just showed up. Yet, even after Sam had told her not to trust him, Genesis had wanted to give him the benefit of the doubt. But that ended the other day in the parking structure when he showed his true colors and then asked for money.

Then he betrayed me.

She never would've guessed that he was capable of physically hurting her. It was out of character, but was it? So much time had passed between them. It was clear that Genesis didn't know the man he had become.

I know now.

Then there was Noah. The look on his face and in his eyes when he saw what Ronnie had done to her would be forever branded in Genesis's mind. Devastation, fear, and even anger had seeped from his pores from the moment he opened her car door until she fell asleep on the way to his house.

But he never left her side, not even during the doctor's exam. He was right there ready to fight anyone who didn't treat her right. That only made Genesis love him that much more.

I don't deserve him. That thought had been plaguing her from the moment she opened her eyes this morning. She had too much baggage, and when she told him about her past, he'd probably want nothing else to do with her.

She didn't want him to know... at least not everything.

Genesis huffed out a breath and glanced around his bedroom—her favorite room in the house. It was a calming space, which was what she needed right now.

The color scheme was beige and brown with touches of gold. The space was lavishly decorated but soothing. On one side of the room were leather panels that covered the wall behind the king-size bed and headboard. Two large nightstands were on either side. Across from the bed was a breathtaking fireplace with a flat-screen television mounted above it.

Every inch of the space reminded her of Noah. Calming. Comfortable. Luxurious. Despite his wealth, he didn't throw around money, but it would be clear to anyone that he liked nice things.

The bedroom door swung open, and Genesis's heart kicked against her chest as her gaze locked onto Noah.

The man was beautiful.

He really should've pursued a career in modeling or acting. He was straight-up eye candy. He even made the old, ratty blue T-shirt, which she vowed to toss one day, look good.

The garment stretched across his broad shoulders, hugged his muscular biceps, and was tight enough to highlight his flat abs. He didn't have a lick of fat anywhere on him. She might not be at her best physically, but she still wanted to run her hands over every inch of his tempting body. Then she wanted to feel him buried between her...

"How do you feel?" Noah asked, and Genesis almost groaned as she squeezed her legs together to tamp down the sudden throb between her thighs.

"I feel okay," she croaked, then cleared her throat. "I'm just..." *Horny, sex-starved, and I want you more than I want that green smoothie you're carrying*, she thought but didn't say out loud.

"Hungry probably," he said. He handed her the smoothie and a banana. "I figured with the swelling you might need soft foods."

Her shoulders drooped. Yep, he was definitely too good for her. "Thank you for everything," she mumbled and sipped from the straw that was sticking out of the smoothie. After drinking almost half of it, she set the glass on the nightstand next to the banana.

With his Hydro Cell water bottle in hand, Noah climbed onto the bed next to her.

Genesis adjusted her long braids to make sure that they still covered most of her face. As if knowing that she was trying to keep him from zoning in on the swelling, Noah reached out and tucked a few of the braids behind her ear.

"Don't hide from me, Gen. You're still the most beautiful woman in the world."

His words were spoken with such conviction, she almost believed him. But Genesis had seen the damage Ronnie had done. Even with her dark skin, discoloration could be detected, and though the swelling had gone down some, her face was still puffy.

Noah sat back against the cloth headboard and crossed his legs at the ankles. "When did you start carrying a gun?" he asked out of the blue. "I guess the most important question is, do you have a permit, and do you know how to use the weapon?"

"Yes, to the last two questions, and I started carrying a couple of years ago. I almost got mugged when I was leaving work late one night," she said of her previous job. "Had it not been for two women who were leaving a restaurant across the street from the building, I don't know what would've happened. They saw me trying to fight the guy off, and one went to get help while the other came over to help me.

"I was so scared, and by the time I got home, I decided that I needed to learn to protect myself. I took a self-defense class, and I purchased a gun."

Noah nodded, but she didn't miss how hard he was gripping the water bottle in his hand. "I'm glad you know how to defend yourself. Now, I need to know what's going on between you and Ronnie," he said without preamble.

Not knowing where to start, she explained how Ronnie had dropped back into her life a month ago. She didn't leave anything out when she told him about their first meeting. She also told him about his phone calls and how she eventually blocked his number. Then there was the meeting in the parking garage.

"I never wanted you to meet Ronnie, and I didn't want him anywhere near you. Then after the other day in the parking structure, I feared he'd somehow try to extort money from you. Noah, I don't know him like I used to. He was my past, and that's what I've told him. I don't want him to be a part of my future." A future with you, she wanted to say but didn't.

At least she hoped that she and Noah could have a future, but his silence said otherwise. Served her right. This conversation was overdue, and though she hoped that he'd be willing to give her another chance, she understood if he didn't. He was a grown-ass man. No way would he tolerate being with a woman who kept secrets. Nor should he.

This was just another sign that he was out of her league. He's already been where she's still trying to get to. Why would he put up with her when he could have any woman he wanted?

Because he loves you, a small voice inside her head said. *He loves you.*

"That's why you said no to my proposal," Noah said as a statement more than a question. "You were trying to get rid of him."

It was more than that, but she said, "Yes. Showing up out of the blue, he caught me off guard."

"Okay. I get that, but let's start from the beginning. Tell me about you guys in foster care."

"When I was fourteen, I was placed at the same foster home as Ronnie and Samantha. I was scared, sad, and just hated to have to be moved again. Not that the previous place was anything to write home about, but I had gotten used to being there.

"Anyway, when I arrived at the new foster home, me and Samantha hit it off immediately." Genesis's heart squeezed at the memory. Sam had welcomed her with open arms, as if she was the mother and Genesis was her child. "It was the same with Ronnie, but different. He wasn't as loving as Sam, but he was so protective of me. Not in a sexual way, but like a real brother."

Genesis could've sworn Noah growled under his breath.

"As I got older, boys started taking notice, but Ronnie had made it his mission that none of them would get close to me. In high school, he had even beat up a guy who was bullying me. No matter the situation, he was always there, looking out for me."

Genesis shared other examples of who Ronnie was to her back then. The more she recalled, the more her heart hurt. She understood why he thought she owed him, or why he might've thought she'd betrayed him by not coming up with the money for him. But any respect she might've had for him was gone the moment he put his hands and feet on her. For that, she would never forgive him.

"I get that he was your protector at one time," Noah said with an edge in his voice, "but what changed?"

"Everything changed when he got arrested for armed robbery weeks after he turned eighteen. Then he spent sixteen years in prison." Genesis bit down on her lip, struggling with how much to tell him, but there were some parts he needed to know. "Ronnie robbed the convenience store... because of me."

"Wait. What?" Noah turned to face her, and suddenly Genesis didn't want to tell him any more. When she went mute, he said, "Tell me. I need to know what this guy has over you."

Unable to look him in the eyes, she fiddled with the sheet that was covering her bare legs.

"I was in high school and scheduled to graduate, but I couldn't afford my senior fees. It might not seem like a big deal to you, but it meant everything to me to be able to walk across that stage. I couldn't do it without a cap and gown."

She swiped at a rogue tear that slipped down her cheek, and Noah handed her a Kleenex from the box on the nightstand.

"I also wanted a class ring. I had some money from my part-time job at a restaurant but not enough. I was a hundred dollars short. I asked my foster mother for the money, and she claimed the State barely paid enough for her to feed me, and that I was on my own for luxuries."

Noah squeezed her hand. Despite the crap that she'd brought to his doorstep, he was still showing her support.

"What does all that have to do with Ronnie?"

"He had just aged out of foster care, but he kept in touch. He picked me up from school one day, and on the way home, I was telling him about what was going on. He told me that he might be able to help me out."

She explained how a few days after they'd talked, Ronnie had robbed a store. No one died, but he had beat up the clerk and stole money from the register. Later on that night, he was apprehended and charged.

Genesis had been devastated, especially when he told her that he'd done it for her. Based on past experience, she knew he would come up with the money, but she never asked him to steal it.

"So, Ronnie is claiming that you owe him because he robbed a store, with a gun, so that he could steal money for you?"

Genesis stared down at her hands that were folded in her lap. It was a little more to it than that, but she couldn't tell him the rest... not yet. Maybe not ever.

"Yes," she said. "He spent years in prison... because of me."

BULLSHIT.

Noah didn't think she was lying, but Genesis wasn't telling him the whole story. Why, was the question.

Frustration simmered below the surface, and it was taking all his control not to insist that she tell him everything. Noah wanted the information to come from her. He wanted her to be the one who told him about her history with Ronnie. But since she wouldn't... or couldn't, he'd have to get answers on his own.

When she tried to fight a yawn, he leaned over and placed a lingering kiss against her temple. Her fresh scent of vanilla and lavender from her shower earlier filled his nostrils, and he was tempted to pull her close and bury his nose against her neck.

There would be time for that later, but right now, there was something he needed to take care of.

"Try to get some sleep, and I'll check on you later," he said.

After helping her get settled under the covers, Noah strolled out of the room on a mission. He wanted answers, and he wanted them now.

Chapter Eleven

"Well, what Genesis told you about Ronnie was true," Ashton said through the phone line as Noah slipped his earbuds into his ear.

This morning, after he and Genesis talked, he had called his brother for help. He wanted as much information on Ronnie as possible. Not that he didn't trust Genesis, but whatever secrets she was keeping was eating him up.

"What your woman probably didn't tell you is that Ronnie had been in foster care since he was three. There's no record of a father, and his mother was a teenage mom. She dropped him off at a police station when he was two, and it's as if she fell off the face of the earth. We haven't been able to find anything on her."

Damn. Hearing stories like Ronnies and Genesis made Noah appreciate his family even more. It was because of Genesis that he planned to start a non-profit to address some of the needs of foster kids. He couldn't relate to what they went through, but he could do his part to possibly give them a better life.

"He was an average student throughout school, and then he got picked up a couple of weeks after he turned eighteen. He was telling the truth about being released a little over four months ago. We're still trying to get information on where he works."

Noah paced behind his desk. "What about his parole officer? Has he been in contact with him?"

"*She* saw him a couple of days ago and agreed to give us a heads up if he checks in."

Ashton explained that he didn't tell Ronnie's parole officer about the attack since Genesis didn't want to make an official report about the incident. But when or if he showed up, his PO agreed to give Ashton a call.

"Thanks, man. Keep me posted. In the meantime, I need another favor. I want everything you can find on Genesis." Noah's chest tightened at the thought of going behind her back for information. He loved the woman more than he thought possible, but this had to be done. "My HR department did a background check on her when she was hired, but I want you to do a deep dive into her background."

His brother released a long whistle. "Are you sure about this?" Ashton asked. "Because you might not like what we find."

Noah stood at the patio door in his home office. He was almost positive that he wasn't going to like whatever they found, but what else could he do? Genesis was still keeping secrets.

Thoughts ran rapidly through his mind as he gazed out at his beautifully manicured yard that was enclosed with a wrought iron fence and numerous trees. His home was located in Johns Creek, a suburb of Atlanta, and sat on an acre lot. The side yard that he was looking out over normally offered a calming view with the large, gurgling waterfall fountain and a rose garden on each side of it. But currently, he felt everything but calm.

"Noah? You still there?" Ashton's voice boomed through Noah's earbuds.

"Yeah, and to answer your question about me wanting you to dig into her background, I'm not sure. But I need to know what she's hiding. Otherwise, I can't help her with whatever's going on, and I can't protect her." And that was his number one goal.

He wasn't sure if Genesis was holding back the truth because she was in danger. Maybe someone had threatened to hurt her if she said anything. Or what if she was being evasive because she was protecting someone?

What if it's me she's protecting? he thought.

Genesis had already mentioned that she hadn't wanted Ronnie anywhere near him for fear he'd try to extort money somehow. Noah could see that, but his gut told him there was more to it. Noah had assured her more than once that there was nothing he wouldn't do for her. What if she still didn't believe him? Or what if she thought that he would leave her at the first sign of trouble?

"I want to know everything. Dig deep enough that you find out how many cavities she has."

His brother chuckled.

Noah didn't know what they'd find, but the only way he and Genesis could move forward is if he knew all her secrets. Good and bad.

"Okay, if you're sure," Ashton said, resignation in his tone.

"I'm positive."

"All right. We'll dig deeper."

"Good. Thanks."

"Oh, and Gen's car was checked out. There were no GPS trackers on her vehicle. So, we have to assume Ronnie followed her to the grocery store."

That news sent a chill down Noah's spine. Who knew how long the guy had been trailing her? Was it just for the money? Or was there something else that Ronnie wanted from her?

"One of us will drop the car off at your place later this evening," Ashton said. "And one more thing. I think this goes without saying, but maybe hold off on another marriage proposal."

Before Noah could respond, Ashton disconnected the call. *Yeah, that's probably good advice... for now.*

DAYS LATER, NOAH SAT in his office reviewing a contract from his legal department. It looked like he was finally going to close this deal that had been in the works for almost six months. His firm, G-spark Engineering, was partnering with another engineering company that manufactured missiles. His team would help redesign a sensor for a missile defense system.

Noah had just finished reading the page that outlined the deadlines when his phone rang. He lifted his cell from the desk and glanced at the screen. *Ashton.* Just the person he'd been waiting to hear from. It had been three days, and he hoped they'd found Ronnie. He also hoped that they'd found out whatever Genesis was hiding.

Things between him and Genesis were comfortable, and they had gotten into a good routine. Their only disagreement had come when she told him that she needed to work while he wanted her to rest. It wasn't that she wanted to go to the office, but she insisted that she needed to put finishing touches on the Juneteenth event.

It was clear that she was afraid to go back to the office, and Noah didn't want her out of his sight. They compromised. He set up an office space with everything she needed in the guest room, which was where she was now.

"Hey. What's up, man?" Noah said when he answered the phone.

"A couple of Laz's contacts came through," Ashton said. "We haven't found Ronnie yet, but we know where he lives. He's been staying with some guy he attended high school with, and the apartment is near your Midtown office building."

"So, it's possible that Ronnie ran into Genesis by chance that first day near the coffee shop," Noah said more to himself than Ashton.

"It's possible."

Ashton confirmed that Ronnie did indeed work at a garage, but the owner hadn't seen him in days. Neither had the parole officer.

"We have some of our guys sitting on the garage and the apartment but, so far, no Ronnie. Something else we learned that your woman may not know is that Ronnie was connected to three other robberies before he was caught that last time. He also used to run with a two-bit drug dealer before going to prison. We're looking into whether they've reconnected."

Robberies, drugs, it was a miracle that Genesis hadn't gotten caught in the middle of Ronnie's mess before or even now.

"What about Genesis? What have you found?"

Ashton sighed loudly, and Noah braced himself for whatever was coming.

"There's more between your woman and her foster brother."

Unease crept through Noah, and he stood rubbing his forehead. "More like what?"

"Ronnie wasn't the only one arrested that night. Genesis was arrested too."

That news was like taking a two-by-four upside the head. Out of all the scenarios that jockeyed inside of Noah's mind, that hadn't been one of them. Why hadn't she told him?

"Was she convicted?" Impatience rattled inside Noah as he tried to come to grips with the news.

"No. She was still a minor and didn't do any time thanks to Ronnie. By the way, her file was sealed. So, you didn't hear any of this from me."

"Yeah, okay." Noah started pacing as he ran his hand over his head but stopped. "How was she involved?"

After a slight hesitation, Ashton said, "She was the getaway driver."

"What?" Noah roared. "No way. There's no way in hell she could've been involved. I don't believe that shit!" And he wouldn't believe it unless he heard it directly from her. But... "Say if Genesis was involved, why wasn't she arrested?" Noah asked, then glanced up to find her standing in the doorway to his office.

Her braids were in a messy bun on top of her head, and she wore one of his dress shirts that stopped at her knees. Noah couldn't tell if she was wearing anything beneath it, but his traitorous body jolted to attention. This was the worst time to be lusting after her but tell that to his body. She looked tempting as hell.

But it was her wide eyes and mouth hanging open that brought him back to reality. She stood frozen in place while holding a large bowl of popcorn, and he knew that this time when they talked, he'd get the full story.

"Ash, let me give you a call back."

Noah disconnected and set his cell phone on his desk.

"Seems like there's more to Ronnie's arrest than you told me."

Chapter Twelve

After a slight hesitation, Genesis moved farther into the room. "You might not believe me, but I just got off the phone with Samantha. I told her that if you and I will ever have a future, I have to tell you everything."

She eased down on the sofa in his office, and his chest tightened. Though she was mostly healed, every time he looked at her, he was reminded of what that asshole did to her. Yet, she survived. She protected herself, but what if Ronnie had done something worse? What if she would've died from her injuries? Noah would've lost her for good.

That thought was sobering as Noah sat next to her and slipped his arm around her. He eased her closer and placed a kiss against her temple.

"Tell me what happened that night of the robbery." When she didn't immediately respond, he continued. "I had Ashton look into him. Imagine my surprise when he learned that you had been arrested that night too. How is it that he went to jail, and you didn't?"

"I was driving," she said, and her voice shook. "But I swear I didn't know Ronnie was going to rob that store, and I didn't know he had a gun."

"How is that possible if you were driving the getaway car?" Noah tried to keep the accusatory tone out of his voice, but it was impossible. He might've been crazy in love with this woman, but he didn't like people lying to him, especially her.

"My foster mother had to work that night, and after she left, Ronnie called. He asked if I wanted to practice driving. I had my permit but no one to teach me to drive, except for him."

Noah hated that she grew up the way she had. It gutted him every time he learned more about her time in foster care. It also made him appreciate his parents and the way he was raised. Their lives hadn't been perfect, but he had no doubt that they loved him and his siblings.

"After we drove around an empty parking lot, he had me drive through neighborhoods."

When she stopped talking, Noah leaned back slightly and glanced down at her.

"Genesis, look at me," he said. When she did, pretty brown eyes stared into his, and his heart squeezed. "If there's a chance for us, there can't be any secrets. You have to trust me enough to know that I love you more than anything, but I can't handle lies or half truths. If I vow to always be honest with you, I need that same respect."

"I know, and I'm so sorry. I never wanted to keep anything from you, but I was afraid."

"Afraid of what?"

"Afraid of losing you. I have worked my butt off to create a good life for myself, but then Ronnie returned and so did my past mistakes. I didn't want anyone to know, especially not you. I—I didn't want you to think less of me. I am so sorry."

She started crying, and Noah held her until her sobs quieted. He understood her need to walk away from her past, but not at the expense of their relationship. They couldn't have any secrets.

"Finish telling me about that night," he said gently. "No more secrets between us."

She nodded against his chest and wiped her eyes with the back of her hand.

"On the way back to the house, he told me to stop by this convenience store. Since there weren't many cars in the lot, he told me to pull up sideways to the door and sit tight. He might've been gone five minutes, and then he jumped into the passenger seat and said, 'Go! Go!' Go!'. Even then, I didn't think much of it. I drove off.

"When we returned to the house, we sat in the car talking. I don't know how long we were out there, but when I looked in the car's rearview mirror, I saw flashing blue lights. Then two other police cars showed up.

"Ronnie had once told me that if you're ever pulled over and more than one cop shows up, somebody's going to jail. I knew then that something had happened at that store and couldn't believe Ronnie hadn't said anything."

Noah listened as she told him about how terrified she'd been and that she kept asking Ronnie, *"What did you do?"*. He finally told her that he had robbed the store and that everything he'd done that night was for her. He claimed to be getting the money she needed for school.

Noah hated the bastard, but one good thing he did that night was tell Genesis not to say anything without a lawyer present.

"There had been cameras inside and outside of the store," Genesis continued. "Everything that happened was on video, including me driving away from the scene. There had even been a photo that showed me in the driver's seat."

Genesis shook her head and huffed out a breath.

"I thought I was going to jail. I told the lawyer that had been appointed to me the truth, but it was my word against what the cops saw on video."

"Damn, baby. I'm so sorry for what you went through. How was it that you got off?"

"Ronnie." She sighed loudly. "In his statement, he told them that I didn't know anything about the robbery before or after. He acted alone. For the longest, I felt guilty because he robbed that store because of me. He did so much for me back then."

"I get that he did a lot for you, but sweetheart, there's something you should know. That night Ronnie got arrested was a long time coming."

Noah shared everything Ashton told him about Ronnie and watched various emotions play out on Genesis's beautiful face. His heart ached for what she went through as a child, but he was proud of the woman she had become.

"I had no idea. He was always kind and generous towards me," she said, shaking her head.

"So, no more feeling guilty about being the reason for Ronnie's incarceration," Noah said and kissed the side of her head. "Also, thanks for telling me what happened."

"I'm sorry I didn't tell you sooner." She turned to better face him. "I love you, Noah. I was afraid that if I told you, I'd lose you."

Noah lifted her chin with the pad of his finger and forced her to look at him. "My love for you is unconditional." He caressed her cheek, careful of where she'd been hit even though the swelling was practically gone. "We all have things in our past that we're not proud of, but no more secrets."

Genesis gave him a watery smile, and it was as if the sun had come out after a rainy day. "No more secrets," she repeated.

Noah lowered his head and covered her luscious lips with his. The kiss started out gentle, but he increased the pressure as hunger for her drove him. Though Genesis hadn't been out of his sight in days, there had still been a distance between them. That was changing tonight. He wanted her so bad, he physically ached, and by the response to his kiss, she was feeling the same way.

Noah lifted her onto his lap so that she straddled him, and as he devoured her mouth, spirals of ecstasy charged to every cell in his body. The woman had such an effect on him, and Noah couldn't think straight while she was grinding against him.

Instead of undoing the buttons on the shirt, he lifted it over her head and tossed it to the floor. His need for her skyrocketed at the sight of her exposed breasts and the lace thong.

He palmed her bare ass and held her close. "God, this body," he murmured, admiring her full breasts before taking a nipple into his mouth. He feasted on it, then moved to the next one as desire pulsed through him.

The sensual sounds she was making as she ground against his dick had him hard as granite, and Noah couldn't wait to reunite their bodies.

Genesis scurried off his lap, and while she hurried out of her thong, he made quick work of unbuckling his jeans. But her bouncing breasts distracted him. Noah's mouth watered, and his jeans were barely past his hips when she climbed back on top of him.

The situation would've been funny if his dick wasn't standing at attention, pulsing, throbbing, and needing to be buried inside of her.

"I want you so bad," she mumbled and shocked the hell out of him when she lifted, then slid down on his shaft.

Noah's eyes slammed shut, and he sucked in a breath as he gripped her hips. Damn, she felt incredible as her tightness squeezed around him. When he reopened his eyes, she was smiling at him.

"My beautiful woman," he said as their bodies moved in perfect sync while he thrust into her. With each stroke, her breasts were bouncing in his face. Noah couldn't help but latch on to one of her nipples and suck her hard while driving in and out of her.

"Aww, baby," she moaned as they picked up speed, soaring higher and higher until Genesis lost it. "Noah!" She screamed her release, and her inner muscles squeezed his dick while her body shuddered in response.

Noah continued pounding into her, going deeper with each thrust until a hot tide of passion sent him tumbling over a proverbial cliff. He cursed under his breath and held his arms around her so tightly he feared that he would crush her. His orgasm rocked him to his core and he collapsed back against the sofa with her.

"Wow," Genesis murmured. Her head rested on his shoulder while his chest heaved.

Sex between them had always been good, but each time they... His body stiffened. "Oh shit," Noah grumbled and squeezed his eyes tight.

Shit. Shit. Shit. He never forgot to use a condom. Never. Until now.

"Gen..."

"I know. Condom." She was still panting and chuckled.

"I'm sorry, sweetheart," Noah said even though she was on the pill. They had long ago established that they were both clean, but they'd still been using condoms.

"Don't be," Genesis said and lifted her head. Her pretty brown eyes sparkled with love and mischief. "I couldn't wait, and it was amazing. Now I can't wait to do it again... upstairs... in your big bed."

HOURS LATER, GENESIS lay wrapped in Noah's strong arms. The past week had her on an emotional rollercoaster, but she was beyond happy that there were no longer secrets between her and Noah. It felt as if a weight had been lifted off her shoulders.

She caressed his chest as his light snores met her ears. God, she was so happy that they were still a couple, but she had to remind herself. Just because Noah still loved her and the sex was amazing, it didn't mean he'd still want to marry her.

Genesis hoped he did because she wanted another chance to say yes.

Chapter Thirteen

Just relax. Everything is going to be great, Genesis told herself as she stood in front of the full-length mirror in her evening gown. She had taken extra care in dressing tonight, wanting to look as beautiful as Noah always made her feel. Her micro braids were twisted into an elegant updo, and her makeup was flawless. Diamonds, a gift from Noah on her birthday the month before, dripped from her earlobes and hung around her neck.

Genesis slid her hand down the front of the sleeveless, peach-colored dress with rhinestones adorning the bodice. It hugged her upper body while the lower half, made of chiffon fabric, flared out and revealed a deep, peekaboo split that exposed her left leg whenever she took a step,

It was the night of the Juneteenth gala, and though she was looking forward to attending, she was glad the planning for it was done. It had been a long few months, but it was the last couple of weeks that wore her out. Between coordinating the event and dealing with the fallout of the situation with Ronnie, she needed a vacation.

Ronnie was still in the wind. Out there somewhere where no one could find him. Genesis hoped they'd never see him again, but Noah doubted it. He was counting on Ronnie returning to finish what he'd started—an attempt to get quick cash.

"Breathe in. Breathe out," she mumbled on a shaky breath just as the bedroom door swung open.

"Sweetheart, we gotta get..." Noah's words trailed off as his gaze gobbled her up.

But while he was checking her out, Genesis allowed her eyes to scan over his handsome form. Noah often dressed like a man with money, and he could make a ratty T-shirt and jeans look amazing, but in a tuxedo? The man was mouthwatering *fiiine*.

The tailored, navy-blue tuxedo jacket molded over his broad shoulders and wide chest. He wore a matching bowtie and a white shirt beneath it. And it was impossible to miss the sparkling, diamond cufflinks peeking out below the sleeve of his jacket.

Genesis's gaze went lower and landed on the shiny Ferragamos on his feet. Yep, like usual, the man looked like money.

"You are absolutely stunning," Noah said as he crossed the room toward her. "There's a part of me that wants to take you to the gala just so that I can show you off and tell the world that you're mine." He stopped in front of her and slid his arm around her waist, then pulled her close. "But the other part of me wants to strip you out of this sexy ass dress, love on your luscious body, and have you screaming my name over and over again until you're hoarse."

Genesis couldn't help but laugh as her cheeks heated. "Maybe I'll let you give it your best shot when we get home."

She startled herself by calling his place home. It felt right on so many levels, but eventually, her life would go back to normal, and she'd have to return to her humble abode.

But for tonight, she planned on enjoying the evening with the man she loved.

She reached up and straightened his bowtie. "For now, though, we're going to this event because I put my heart and soul into creating the best gala and silent auction that you've ever hosted. No way am I missing it. Not even for the most handsome man in the world."

Noah flashed her a sexy grin. "In that case, we should head out before I lose control and go with my idea of stripping you. But first, there's something I've wanted to do from the moment I walked in here."

He crushed her to him, claimed her mouth, then slipped his tongue between her lips. All rational thoughts left Genesis's mind as she gave in to the passion of his kiss. She could stay like this forever, but if they were going to make it to the event on time, one of them needed to put a halt to their tongue aerobics.

She groaned, then pressed a hand to his chest and reluctantly broke off their kiss. "The faster we get out of here, the sooner we can return," she said and smiled at Noah when he huffed out an exaggerated breath.

"Fine but be prepared to pick up where we left off."

Hours later, Genesis sat at the table with some of Noah's family and friends and Samantha and her date. Noah stood at the podium giving his annual speech.

"I trust that you're enjoying your evening of great food and wonderful entertainment. Though the night isn't over, I wanted to take a few minutes to thank you for attending," he said. "Each year, the Mr. Black organization sponsors community Juneteenth celebrations all over the country. This is my last year as Mr. Black Atlanta, but this won't be my last time hosting this worthwhile event."

Cheers went up around the room, and just when Genesis thought she couldn't be prouder of him, she was proven wrong. She loved that despite being swamped with work, Noah made time to give back to the community. Whether it was volunteering at a food bank or raising money for causes he believed in, he made time.

"I love celebrating Juneteenth not only because of what the holiday represents but also because it's an opportunity to educate people about a special time in history. As usual, our organizers did a fabulous job planning this event, but I especially liked the Juneteenth trivia booth located in the lobby.

"Like me, I saw a lot of you surprised at how much you didn't know about the holiday. Like what is the Emancipation of Proclamation, and why did it take over two years for it to be enforced in Texas?"

Genesis smiled as the three hundred people in attendance started talking amongst themselves, including those at her table. Seemed Noah's mother was the only one at their table who knew the answer to both questions. The Emancipation of Proclamation was a proclamation that declared all slaves be freed. It had taken years for that to happen because emancipation couldn't be enforced in the Confederate states until after the civil war.

Joy bubbled inside Genesis as conversation and a few debates regarding other trivia questions flowed throughout the huge ballroom. It took Noah several attempts to regain everyone's attention.

"Another reason why I enjoy hosting this event is because it also brings attention to needs in our communities," he continued. "This year, one hundred percent of the money raised will go toward supporting Black communities. Specifically young adults aging out of foster care," he said, and his gaze landed on Genesis.

Heat spread through her body as her heart swelled in her chest. Not just because he was looking at her with such love, but also because this was a cause dear to her too. After leaving foster care, she struggled with basic needs, such as housing. Her minimum income barely put food on the table, and her desire to attend college had been nothing but a dream. But with help from various nonprofit organizations and state-funded programs, she survived, thrived, and her biggest dream became a reality.

Once Noah and the others were done with their speeches, everyone mingled.

"Dance with me," Noah said and extended his hand to Genesis.

She allowed him to guide her to the crowded dance floor as the band played "Still" by Tamia, one of Genesis's favorite songs. She wondered if Noah had anything to do with the song choice.

"You and your team outdid yourselves this year," he said as he held her close, and they swayed to the music. "You thought of everything."

"Thank you, but I had a ton of help. I enjoyed your speech, even if you went over the fifteen-minute limit."

He flashed her a sheepish grin, and her heart did a jig.

"I'd say I'm sorry, but you know when I start talking about various causes and all that the Mr. Black organization does for the community, I get carried away."

"I know, and I love how passionate you are about anything you get involved with."

"Including you," he said and kissed her deeply as if trying to show just how passionate he was when it came to her. Genesis felt it. She felt his love from the top of her head to the tips of her toes, and she couldn't be happier.

When the kiss ended, Noah spun her out and then pulled her back against his muscular body. Before long, he was gliding her around the dance floor, as if they danced together all the time.

Genesis laughed at his antics and felt freer than she'd felt in a long time. Or maybe it had everything to do with there not being any more secrets between them.

Either way, joy and happiness flowed through her, and she couldn't wait to see what the future held for her and Noah.

Chapter Fourteen

"Home sweet home," Noah said when he pulled into his garage and shut off the car.

He glanced at Genesis who was sitting in the passenger seat, looking more relaxed than she had in weeks. Reaching for her hand, he brought it to his lips and kissed the back of her fingers.

She smiled at him, and he felt like the luckiest man on the planet.

"You are the most amazing woman I've ever met. Thanks for making me look good tonight, and the gala was incredible."

She leaned over and kissed him. "I'm glad you enjoyed it."

"I did. Now, let's go inside, and I'll draw you a nice warm bubble bath. Then I'll wash your back for you."

Genesis laughed. "Sounds good to me."

They climbed out of the car and headed to the door that led into the house. Noah pushed the button to let down the garage door, but on its way down, it suddenly stopped.

He glanced over his shoulder, and his blood froze in his veins.

"What are you..." Genesis's words trailed off when she saw what he was looking at.

Ronnie... and he had a gun pointed at Genesis. "Well, don't just stand there, let's take this party inside." He motioned with his gun. "Open the door nice and slowly. Try any funny stuff, and she's dead."

Noah gripped Genesis's hand. "I'll give you whatever you want, just let her leave," he said.

He didn't know how the bastard got onto the property, but it was only a matter of time before help arrived. There were sensors strategically placed and outdoor cameras. Authorities would be notified.

"Genesis, toss your purse over there," Ronnie said, nodding toward the front of the car, as if Noah hadn't spoken. "Can't have you pulling a gun on me again. You look very pretty by the way."

Genesis tightened her hand around Noah's but did as Ronnie said and tossed her purse.

Ronnie moved forward. "Now, let's go inside."

Noah unlocked the door with one hand and held on to Genesis with the other. The moment he pushed the door open, the house alarm blared.

"Hurry up. Turn it off!" Ronnie roared, and Noah did, but instead of entering his usual security code, he entered his ambush code that would go directly to Supreme Security.

Ronnie might've found a way onto the property, but he'll be escorted off soon.

"Now move!" he demanded, pointing the gun toward the kitchen. "I don't have all day."

"What do you want?" Noah asked as they entered the kitchen. He wrapped his arm around Genesis and pulled her against his body. Pretending to kiss her, he whispered, "Be ready to drop to the floor."

Ronnie kept his gun aimed at Genesis. So far, she hadn't said anything, but she was gripping Noah's hand tight enough to break bones.

"First, I want Genesis to step away from you."

"Nah, man," Noah said, easing his body in front of Genesis. "What you're not going to do is point that gun at my woman. I'll do what you want, but she stays by my side."

Ronnie released a harsh laugh. "That's what I hate about you rich motherfuckers. You think just because you have money that you're running shit. Not tonight, rich boy. I'm calling the shots!" he spat and moved within striking distance.

"I want fifty Gs transferred to this account." He held up a slip of paper. "I also want whatever cash you have on you. Actually, give the cash to Genesis, and she'll give it to me. I don't trust your ass."

"Ronnie, don't do this," Genesis pleaded. "Just leave, and we'll forget you were ever here."

Ronnie laughed as if she'd told him the funniest joke. "Oh, sweet, naive, Genesis. I'm not going anywhere. Either your boyfriend gives me what I want, or I'm taking what's his. Come here!"

Ronnie yanked Genesis's arm and pulled her to him causing her to stumble and fall.

"Gen!" Noah yelled and lunged for Ronnie. "Run, baby. Get out of here!"

He slammed into the man, knocking the gun from his grasp seconds before they both crashed into a wall and then to the floor.

Rage rippled through Noah. He smashed his fist into Ronnie's jaw and did it again, and again.

But Ronnie gave as good as he got, jabbing his elbow into Noah's temple, and throwing him off balance. They rolled around on the floor, both trying to get the upper hand. The guy was moving so much, Noah struggled to get ahold of him.

"You thought you had me, rich boy? I'm from the streets, man!" Ronnie barked and gripped the collar of Noah's shirt before punching him in the side of the head. He swung a few more times, but Noah kept moving, causing him to hit air.

They exchanged punches back and forth, until one of Noah's landed in Ronnie's face, giving Noah the break he needed.

"I got your rich boy," Noah growled and straddled the guy. He crashed his fist into the man's eye and felt a bit of satisfaction when Ronnie cried out. Not giving him a chance to recover, Noah kept hitting him in the face.

"Get off me!" Ronnie growled and threw a punch but missed.

Noah wrapped his hands around the man's neck and squeezed. "You were a *dead man* the moment you put your hands on my woman!" Noah roared. "Then you thought you could steal from me?"

Noah heard a commotion behind him, but he didn't release his hold on Ronnie who was gasping for air and slapping at Noah's arms. He banged the man's head against the floor, wanting the jerk to feel the same pain he had inflicted on Genesis.

"Don't you *ever* touch her again!"

"All right, that's enough! Get up." Noah recognized Ashton's voice seconds before his brother hauled him off Ronnie.

Noah shook out of his grasp and glanced around frantically. "Where's Genesis? Gen!" he yelled.

"She's in the family room."

Noah hurried out of the kitchen while officers arrested Ronnie. It seemed there were people everywhere—law enforcement and the men of Supreme Security.

When he reached the opening of his family room, there was a police officer questioning Genesis.

"Noah!" Genesis rushed to him. She wrapped her arms around his waist. "Oh, my God. I'm so glad you're okay." She leaned back without releasing him, and her worried gaze met his. "You're bleeding." She ran her thumb across his bottom lip.

"Ow," he grumbled, then held her close. "Are you okay?"

"Yeah, but you scared me to death. What were you thinking charging at him like that when he had a gun in his hand?" she yelled.

"I was thinking that I wanted to beat his ass for putting his hands on you. Besides, that was nothing."

"Yeah, we used to call him Bone-crusher when we were kids," Ashton said. "Noah was the fighter in the family. I think we all suffered a broken bone or two thanks to him."

Noah chuckled remembering those days. Growing up with three brothers and a sister kept things lively in their household.

He sobered when he glanced down into Genesis's tear-stained face. "You sure you're okay?"

She nodded and laid her head against his chest. Suddenly, he was hit with the fact that he could've lost her tonight.

But you didn't. She's here. She's safe.

For the next hour, Noah's home was a mass of commotion. He had learned that Ronnie snuck onto the property at the same time Noah opened the gate and drove up the long driveway. Now the man was in custody and would spend the rest of his life behind bars. That gave Noah some peace, but jail seemed too good for him.

Once everyone was gone, Noah set the alarm and went to the kitchen to check on Genesis. She was sweeping up glass from the floor and glanced at him.

"Is it over?" she asked, hope swimming in her eyes.

Noah nodded. "It's over."

Epilogue

T*hree weeks later...*
   "You didn't mention that Noah was stopping by," Samantha said when she strolled into the kitchen. "If I had known, I would've made myself scarce."

"What are you talking about?" Genesis asked as she loaded the last dish into the dishwasher. "He's still in Chicago."

Noah had left on a business trip last Friday, to her dismay, and wasn't scheduled to return until this Friday.

"Um, no. Your Mr. One and Only just pulled into the driveway, and considering you look a hot mess, I'm guessing you didn't know."

"What?" Genesis shrieked. "Stall him!"

She made a mad dash to her bedroom and started stripping out of her paint-splattered, cleaning T-shirt and bra before reaching the bathroom. After cleaning all day, she had planned to shower and then curl up with a good book but got distracted. The last thing Genesis expected was for Noah to arrive back in town two days early.

She quickly shimmied out of her short shorts and panties, leaving them in the middle of the bathroom floor.

"This is going to be the quickest shower ever," she mumbled under her breath and hurried into the stall. Within minutes, she was clean and drying off and felt as if she had just run a marathon.

Why am I rushing? Noah should've called to let her know that he was back in town. At least then, she would've been dressed and had a nice dinner prepared. She should be pissed, but she smiled as giddiness bubbled inside of her.

They might've only been a part for a few days, but she had missed him like crazy. He had asked her to travel with him, but she was saving her vacation days for their trip to Hawaii at the end of the summer.

Genesis rubbed scented lotion over her damp body and then rushed out of the bathroom to get dressed, but the moment she stepped across the threshold, she screamed.

"Noah!" She crossed her arms and legs to hide her nakedness. "God, you scared me to death! What are you..." The rest of her words died on her tongue as she realized what was happening. "Ohmigod. Ohmigod. Noah," she whispered, and tears filled her eyes.

He was on one knee holding open a small black velvet box that held the biggest and the prettiest diamond ring she'd ever seen.

"Damn, baby. Now this is how a man likes to return home," he said as his gaze ate her up.

Genesis glanced down at herself. *Oh crap.* "Hold that thought."

She darted back into the bathroom and grabbed a towel to wrap around her body. When she returned, Noah was still on the floor, but on all fours cracking up.

"It's not funny," she said in mock irritation and fought a smile when he dabbed at his eyes with the heel of his hand. "*Noah*, weren't you going to ask me something?"

"God, I love you," he said, still chuckling as he struggled to get back on one knee. He shook his head and grinned at her. "Gen, I can't imagine my life without you in it. I want to have babies with you and grow old with you. I know I botched that last proposal, but my feelings for you haven't changed. If anything, they are stronger than ever. I love you, sweetheart. Will you marry me?"

Joy swirled inside of her as tears trickled down her cheeks, and she bobbed her head. "I love you so much," she said. "Of course, I'll marry you."

She couldn't hold back the squeal that slipped through her lips when he slid the ring onto her finger.

Genesis held her hand out and stared at the ring. "It's gorgeous, honey. Thank you."

She cupped his face and kissed him, then laughed when he unhooked her towel and lifted her off the floor before covering her mouth with his.

"Thank you for saying yes this time," he mumbled against her lips.

"Thank you for asking me again," she responded. "But for the record, your timing is horrible when it comes to marriage proposals."

They fell out laughing, and Genesis knew that he would be her one and only for the rest of her life.

If you enjoyed this book by Sharon C. Cooper,
consider leaving a review on any online book site, review site or
social media outlet.

Next In the Baes of Juneteenth Series...

Thank you for reading Mr. One and Only! I hope you enjoyed Noah and Genesis as much as I enjoyed writing about them. Be sure to grab copies of the complete series. Books in **BOLD** below are connected, and all the books in the series can be read in any order:

Mr. Straight Up No Chaser by Sherelle Green

Mr. Right Now by Sheryl Lister

Mr. Down for Whatever by Elle Wright

Mr. Alpha Undone by Kelsey Green

Mr. Second Best by Angela Seals

Mr. Big Stuff by Aja

Mr. Play for Keeps by Kimmie Ferrell

Mr. Take Me As I Am by Iris Bolling

Mr. On Your Knees by A.C. Arthur

Mr. One and Only by Sharon C. Cooper

Mr. Tall Dark and Unavailable by Tina Martin

Want to know more about Supreme Security (Atlanta's Finest Series) that was mentioned in this story? Visit my website at https://sharoncooper.net/atlanta-s-finest-series

Join Sharon's Mailing List

To get sneak peeks of upcoming stories and to hear about giveaways that Sharon is sponsoring, go to https://sharoncooper.net/newsletter to join her mailing list.

Other Books by Sharon C. Cooper

Atlanta's Finest Series
Vindicated (book 1)
Indebted (book 2)
Accused (book 3)
Betrayed (book 4)
Hunted (book 5)
Tempted (book 6)
Committed (book 7)

Jenkins & Sons Construction Series (Contemporary Romance)
Love Under Contract (book 1)
Proposal for Love (book 2)
A Lesson on Love (book 3)
Unplanned Love (book 4)

Jenkins Family Series (Contemporary Romance)
Best Woman for the Job (Short Story Prequel)
Still the Best Woman for the Job (book 1)
All You'll Ever Need (book 2)
Tempting the Artist (book 3)
Negotiating for Love (book 4)
Seducing the Boss Lady (book 5)
A Love So Strong: A Jenkins Family Reunion (book 6)
Love at Last (Holiday Novella)
When Love Calls (Novella)

MR. ONE AND ONLY

More Than Love (Novella)
Reunited Series (Romantic Suspense)
Blue Roses (book 1)
Secret Rendezvous (Prequel to Rendezvous with Danger)
Rendezvous with Danger (book 2)
Truth or Consequences (book 3)
Operation Midnight (book 4)
Casino Heat (book 5)
Stand Alones
Something New ("Edgy" Sweet Romance)
Legal Seduction (Harlequin Kimani – Contemporary
Romance)
Sin City Temptation (Harlequin Kimani – Contemporary
Romance)
A Dose of Passion (Harlequin Kimani – Contemporary
Romance)
Model Attraction (Harlequin Kimani – Contemporary
Romance)
A Passionate Kiss (Contemporary Romance)
Soul's Desire (Unparalleled Love series)
Show Me (Irresistible Husband series)
His to Protect (Harlequin Romantic Suspense)
His to Defend (Harlequin Romantic Suspense)
Business Not As Usual (Romantic Comedy)
In It to Win It (Romantic Comedy)
Kiss Me (Irresistible Husband – Contemporary Romance)

About the Author

USA Today bestselling author Sharon C. Cooper loves anything involving romance with a happily-ever-after, whether in books, movies, or real life. She writes contemporary romance, as well as romantic suspense and enjoys rainy days, carpet picnics, and peanut butter and jelly sandwiches. Her stories have won numerous awards over the years, and when Sharon isn't writing, she's hanging out with her amazing husband, doing volunteer work, or reading a good book (a romance of course). To read more about Sharon and her novels, visit www.sharoncooper.net[1]

Facebook fan page: http://www.facebook.com/AuthorSharonCCooper21?ref=hl

Twitter: https://twitter.com/#!/Sharon_Cooper1

Goodreads: http://www.goodreads.com/author/show/5823574.Sharon_C_Cooper

Pinterest: https://www.pinterest.com/sharonccooper/

Instagram: https://www.instagram.com/authorsharonccooper/

Bookbub: bookbub.com/profile/sharon-c-cooper

---

1. http://www.sharoncooper.net/

www.ingramcontent.com/pod-product-compliance
Lightning Source LLC
Chambersburg PA
CBHW052010170626
46808CB00007B/2858